"You've got me under some kind of spell," Jake said

"Right back at you," Rachel told him. "I'll see your spell and raise you an incantation or two."

He grinned. "That's what I like about you. You give as good as you get."

She blinked up at him. "Did you just admit you like me?"

"I already admitted we're friends, but it was probably part of that whole spell thing you've got going."

"I see." She slid her hands from his neck, down over the muscular contours of his chest. "Far be it for me to wear out my welcome. I'll just take my spell and go home—"

"The hell you will," he said, tightening his hold.

A sound came from the monitor in her pocket. A little cough and a sneeze.

"Omigosh. *Emma.*"

Dear Reader,

I've put together a list of Silhouette Romance New Year's resolutions to help you get off to a great start in 2004!

• Play along with our favorite boss's daughter's mischievous, matchmaking high jinks. In *Rules of Engagement* (#1702) by Carla Cassidy, Emily Winters—aka the love goddess—is hoping to unite a brooding exec and feisty businesswoman. This is the fifth title in Silhouette Romance's exclusive, six-book MARRYING THE BOSS'S DAUGHTER series.

• Enjoy every delightful word of *The Bachelor Boss* (#1703) by the always-popular Julianna Morris. In this modern romantic fairy tale, a prim plain Jane melts the heart of a sexy playboy.

• Join the fun when a cowboy's life is turned inside out by a softhearted beauty and the tiny charge he finds on his doorstep. *Baby, Oh Baby!* (#1704) is the first title in Teresa Southwick's enchanting new three-book miniseries IF WISHES WERE… Stay tuned next month for the next title in this series that features three friends who have their dreams come true in unexpected ways.

• Be sure not to miss *The Baby Chronicles* (#1705) by Lissa Manley. This heartwarming reunion romance is sure to put a satisfied smile on your face.

Have a great New Year!

Mavis C. Allen
Associate Senior Editor

Please address questions and book requests to:
Silhouette Reader Service
U.S.: 3010 Walden Ave., P.O. Box 1325, Buffalo, NY 14269
Canadian: P.O. Box 609, Fort Erie, Ont. L2A 5X3

Baby, Oh Baby!

Teresa Southwick

if Wishes Were...

SILHOUETTE *Romance*®

Published by Silhouette Books

America's Publisher of Contemporary Romance

To Angie Ray and Marianne Donley—my gratitude
for all the nitpicking. Here's to the power of three.

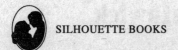 SILHOUETTE BOOKS

ISBN 0-373-19704-7

BABY, OH BABY!

Copyright © 2004 by Teresa Ann Southwick

Printed in U.S.A.

TERESA SOUTHWICK

lives in Southern California with her hero husband, who is more than happy to share with her the male point of view. An avid fan of romance novels, she is delighted to be living out her dream of writing for Silhouette Books.

The fortune-teller said…

The baby you ask for comes with a price.

The promise you make could cost you twice.

If the three born on February twenty-ninth
rub the magic from the lamp and make
a wish—on that day that comes only once
every four years—each shall receive
her most coveted desire.

But there is peril.

Each of the three must see beyond the evident.
Look into the soul of the one her heart
has chosen. Only then will she find
the truth that is hers alone.

Prologue

"**W**hat are the odds of being born on February 29?" Rachel Manning looked at Ashley Gallagher and Jordan Bishop, her two best friends in the world and fellow leap year birthday celebrators.

"If you're the three of us, the chances are one hundred percent," Ashley answered.

Jordan tapped her chin thoughtfully. "When you think about it, the odds of three women remaining friends from the newborn nursery to the present are probably astronomical. We're legendary, like the Three Musketeers."

"Pop quiz," Ashley said. "What was your best birthday?"

"You're such a college girl," Jordan teased. "Although we're twenty-four today, technically we've only had six birthdays, so the question doesn't put a strain on the memory banks.''

"*This* is the best birthday," Ashley said. "How cool is it to be here in New Orleans?"

"I second that." Rachel glanced uneasily over her shoulder. "It's getting late. We should probably head back. I'd like to make a toast to us at a cozy hotel bar."

"Aw, Mom, don't be a party pooper," Ashley teased. "This is my last carefree night. Tomorrow it's back to work and classes. For the next two and a half months I have to gird my loins, or whatever you call it, to get ready for finals and graduation."

"Hallelujah." Jordan grinned.

"Better late than never," Ashley defended herself. "I want to squeeze every last ounce of fun out of tonight. By my calculations, we only have about fifteen minutes left until our birthday is over. And we won't have another official one for four more years." Jordan linked her arms through theirs, urging them forward. "Let's see what kind of trouble we can get into before we get that birthday drink."

That was when Rachel heard someone yelling. Just ahead she saw a woman standing on the sidewalk outside a shop. She was agitated and pointing. "Stop him! Thief! Help!"

Rachel's heart thumped hard against her ribs. Oh, where was that safe hotel bar when you really needed it? People on the sidewalk parted and she saw a slight figure in a black ski cap and dark clothes running straight toward them.

Jordan tugged on their arms, urging them out of the way, which was just fine with Rachel. But if he had a knife or a gun....

Then the thief was directly in front of them and Rachel saw Jordan's foot slide out. As he went down, something fell from his hand and clattered on the walkway at their feet. Jordan bent and grabbed it. Half a second later the guy was up, shooting them a furious look. Rachel braced herself for his attack. But when a siren sounded, he took off around the corner.

"Jordan," Ashley said, her voice breathless, "When you decide to find trouble, you don't waste any time."

"Everyone okay?" Rachel asked. She looked at one then the other of her friends.

"Yeah," Ashley said. "Shouldn't we do something? Call the police? Chase him?"

"He's long gone." Jordan was turning the tarnished brass she'd picked up from side to side. "The only thing we can do is return this. It looks like a lamp, straight out of Aladdin."

Rachel shook her head. "That's your adventurous streak talking. It looks like a glorified gravy boat to me. But obviously that woman wants it back."

Together, they walked toward the waiting woman. She looked like a Gypsy, dressed all in black with a matching bandanna tied pirate style over her dark brown hair.

Jordan held out the recovered object. "Are you all right?"

"Yes." The woman turned the thing over, examining it. "If this had fallen into the hands of someone who abused it…" She shook her head and let out a breath. "I am very grateful."

"It was nothing," Ashley said. "Jordan's big feet are always getting in the way." She grinned when the owner of the big feet in question glared at her.

The Gypsy shook her head. "You shall be rewarded for your courage. Won't you please come inside?"

"I don't know about this, you guys," Rachel said, glancing down at the fog swirling around their feet. It was then she noticed the strange green light glowing inside the shop.

"It's all smoke and mirrors. You need to loosen up and be open to new experiences. Carpe diem. When an opportunity presents itself, seize it with both hands and go along for the ride." Jordan linked her arms through theirs again and tugged them into the shop.

"My name is Faith," the woman said. She turned, holding the dull, dirty brass thing as if it was spun gold. "Each of you must rub the lamp and make a wish."

"I told you it was a lamp," Jordan said.

"Isn't the going rate for a good deed three wishes?" Ashley asked.

Jordan made a tsking noise. "No wonder it's taken you so long to get through college. Do the math. One wish apiece *is* three wishes."

"And one is all you need if it's the right one," the strange woman said.

"Okay. But as the story goes, a genie will appear. What do we do then? One guy? Three women? Do we arm wrestle for a date with him?" Ashley asked.

"No genie," Faith said. "That's very yesterday. But I promise if you wish for your heart's desire, you will be rewarded."

Ashley met Rachel's gaze. "With your track record, it wouldn't be smart to wish for a man. On the off chance your wish comes true."

"No man," Rachel agreed. Every time she'd let herself care, she lost something.

"I don't want a man, either," Jordan commented.

"Good." Ashley nodded emphatically.

"Let's do a group rub," Jordan suggested, taking it from the woman. "We'll wish for the most outrageous things we can think of."

Together they took the lamp and rested it on their palms.

"Feel that?" Rachel asked uneasily. Warmth seemed to emanate from metal she'd expected to be cold. "It feels like it's vibrating."

"You're just shaking." Ashley looked at the lamp. "I'll go first. I wish for money and power." She glanced up and searched their gazes. "What?"

"That's two wishes," Rachel pointed out.

"Power is sort of a subset of money."

As Rachel rubbed her index finger along the curved side of the brass, she thought of the pregnant teenager temporarily sharing her apartment. An emptiness opened up inside her producing an almost painful ache. "I wish I had a baby." She smiled sheepishly at her friends' shocked expressions. "You wouldn't let me wish for a man."

"That's the best outrageous you can do?" Jordan heaved an exaggerated sigh. "I can top you both. I want to be a princess and live in a palace."

"Oo-kay." Rachel laughed. "That's pretty outrageous since you have a better chance of kissing an above average-looking toad than meeting a handsome prince."

But she found herself caught up in the moment and filled with a sense of anticipation. She watched and waited. But nothing happened. Although she hadn't expected anything, she was oddly deflated when that's what she got. So much for three wishes.

"Excellent," Faith said, as she lifted the lamp from their palms.

Rachel rubbed her forehead. "How do you figure?" The Gypsy tilted her head. "Remember, magic works in mysterious ways. Happy birthday to you all."

Stunned, they stared at her for several moments. "How did you know it was our birthday?" Rachel finally asked.

The odd woman smiled mysteriously.

Then a clock chimed midnight.

Chapter One

Through tired, aching eyes, Rachel Manning stared down at the grumpy month-old baby girl, then opened the tabs on the disposable diaper. After capturing the tiny, flailing ankles in one hand, she pulled down the diaper and wrinkled her nose. "Paydirt. No pun intended, Emma. But you're such a sweet, delicate flower, how can you be such a party pooper?"

Whoa. Rachel hadn't thought about that phrase since the night of her birthday celebration in New Orleans when she'd made a wish. She looked down at the infant waving her tiny arms and shook her head. Couldn't be. And even if she believed such a thing was possible, surely her fairy godmother or wish warranty customer service representative could read between the lines.

I want a baby meant finding a man, falling in love

and getting married. A baby would follow after nine months of pregnancy. She wondered if there was a wish complaint department because she had a bone to pick with someone. Several important steps had been skipped.

She shook her head. She was giving way too much credence to that surreal scene. Could a person hallucinate from sleep deprivation? "No way do I believe in magic lamps. I still say it looked like a solid brass gravy boat."

The baby's mewling sounds cranked up and blended into one, single full-blown wail followed by more unhappy squeaking. "It's okay, Em. Don't you worry your pretty head. Didn't I say I'd take care of you? After a certain amount of arm twisting and guilt-tripping," she mumbled.

Rachel had met Holly Johnson at Sweet Spring Hospital where she worked. The pregnant teen went to the obstetrical clinic for her prenatal care. At eighteen, she was released from the state foster care program and Rachel had taken her in. This baby belonged to Holly and her boyfriend Dan Fletcher. Very reluctantly, Rachel had agreed to care for the child, giving the teenagers a chance to find out if the two of them could make a go of it or not. They needed time to make a very adult decision about whether or not to give up this baby.

And Rachel took full responsibility for putting the idea of taking some time away into their heads. But who knew they'd tweak it like this? She'd only agreed to care for the baby after the kids told her Dan's older brother and guardian supported the idea.

But all the logic in the world didn't take away Rachel's feeling that this baby had been left on her doorstep. And she wanted to believe the teens really would come back. Unlike her own parents.

A rusty, familiar pain twisted inside Rachel. Wow, she must really be tired. It was the only explanation for dredging up those old feelings. That was ancient history and she really was *so* over it.

And who cared anyway when this beautiful infant was staring up at her with big innocent eyes. Something she'd never before experienced squeezed tight in the region of her heart. This child needed to be cared for and Rachel intended to do just that. To the best of her ability. Which was, at the moment, slightly handicapped on account of very little sleep.

She finished diapering the tiny girl, then cradled the baby against her shoulder. "Shh, little one," she crooned. "What do you want? You're fed. You've got clean pants. What's wrong?"

She sat on her couch, but that produced another ear-splitting squall that bordered on a pitch only a dog could hear. "Oo-kay."

Instantly, Rachel stood and paced from one end of her ground floor two bedroom apartment to the other, wondering which would wear out first—the rug, the baby or her. Rubbing the infant's tiny back as she walked, she tried to ignore her bone-deep weariness. Did all new mothers do this? How, after the physical rigors of giving birth, did the average woman manage this aerobic exercise?

A sudden knock on the door startled her. It was barely seven o'clock in the morning. Who could possibly— Hope expanded like a balloon inside her.

"Maybe that's your mom," she said to the baby. "She only left yesterday, but I bet she missed you like crazy and couldn't wait for a decent hour to see you.

Besides, she already knows you're a baby and you don't keep decent hours.''

Rachel slid off the security chain and turned the deadbolt, then yanked open the door. But it wasn't Holly Johnson standing there. Not even close. Wrong gender.

"Morning, Rachel." The deep voice never failed to scrape along her nerve endings.

"Jake." Jake Fletcher, the man who rubbed her the wrong way. He also happened to be the baby's uncle. Could this day get any worse?

"Sorry to bother you—" He stared at her. "Good Lord. Are you all right?"

She glanced in the mirror over the small table in her midget-size entry. Yikes! Her blond hair stood up in spikes all over her head. That was bad since she wasn't going for the punk look. The only makeup she had on was what she hadn't had the energy to wash off the night before. Having an infant crying at all hours in a small apartment wasn't conducive to a regular beauty regimen. Beauty, heck. She'd barely managed basic hygiene. And the cherry on the melted sundae that was her life—she was in pajamas. Shorty pajamas. She was practically naked.

"I'm fine." She clutched the baby tighter against her. "What are you doing here?"

"It's about Dan."

"Of course it is. The last time you came to my apartment was when you found out Holly was pregnant and your brother was the father."

"I remember. She'd just been cut loose from her foster home after turning eighteen. And had nowhere to go until you stepped in," he finished, his voice dripping sarcasm.

"I'm not sure what you're implying, Jake. But like

I told you then, I met her at the hospital's prenatal clinic and suggested she stay with me temporarily.''

"So you could help her figure out what state programs might be of help to her," he said dryly.

"It's what I do. I'm a hospital discharge planner. It's my job to know what programs are available to all patients."

"Right."

This guy really fried her grits and he had from the first moment she'd met him. "The last time you showed up on my doorstep you demanded that Holly marry your brother."

"They have a baby. It's the right thing to do," he shot back.

"I'm not going to debate that with you at this hour. By the way, what are you doing here at this hour?" What are you doing here—period—was what she'd wanted to say. But she held back. Then she remembered. "Oh. Right. Dan. What about him?"

"Is he here?"

Uh-oh. He didn't know where Dan was? She had the mother of all bad feelings.

"I haven't seen him," she said truthfully.

"He didn't come by to see Holly and the baby?"

"Yesterday, then he left." With Holly and *not* the baby. And Jake was supposed to know all about this.

"Can I talk to Holly?"

Rachel's protective maternal mode switched into high gear. Holly had been adamantly against leaving the baby with Jake when Rachel had suggested it. And this guy had gotten on her bad side—he'd never been on her good side—since she'd first met him. Because of his perpetual disapproving expression every time he looked at Holly. When he came near her, the teen had clutched Dan's hand. And if Jake spoke to Holly, she seemed to shrink—not easy when her belly had grown large with the baby.

Jake had accompanied Holly and Dan to childbirth classes and hovered like an enforcer, making it plain as the groove in his square jaw that he intended to call the shots in this situation. Rachel believed that one caught more flies with honey than vinegar. The teens had made a mistake. A really big mistake. But they needed direction not a dictator.

"Look, I know this probably isn't the best time," he finally said when she didn't respond to his question.

"What was your first clue? The pajamas?"

One corner of his mouth quirked up. "I mean this in the nicest possible way, but you normally look better."

"Better than what?" She couldn't decide if he'd just paid her a compliment or not. At the moment she looked like something the cat yakked up, but usually she looked better? "What does that mean?"

"Your eyes are bloodshot and the circles underneath practically go to your—" He glanced down to her chest where the baby had relaxed against her, then raised his gaze to hers. "To your knees."

"Obviously you don't know what it's like to be up all night with a newborn," she snapped.

"No, I don't."

Rachel normally didn't snap at people, even ones like him who tried to run the world. In fact, she didn't much care for people who snapped at others. But after being up all hours of the night with a crying baby, snapping came sort of naturally.

It had felt good in fact—right up to the moment she thought she saw a flash of pain in his deep blue eyes.

Now why did she have to go and notice that? She could be wrong. Nothing hurt the Jake Fletchers of the world—the strong, stoic, silent types. The hot, hunky, heartbreaker types. But when she studied him, the way he quickly shuttered the expression, she knew she wasn't wrong. She'd seen that lost look before. More times than she could count. Jordan and Ashley had told her she should quit trying to mother the world. But old habits died hard. Case in point—Holly, her latest maternal mission.

"I'm sorry. That was rude of me to snap at you," she said. "I guess my social skills need a good night's sleep."

"No harm done."

"Okay, good. Let's start over. Come in." She let out a long breath, bracing for the conversation she knew they needed to have.

"Thanks," he said, stepping over the threshold. He shut the door behind him.

"Jake, there's something you need to know—"

"Dan's gone." Jake was holding his black Stetson in his hands, twirling it. "He didn't come home last night."

"I know."

"You do?" Something dark and dangerous shadowed the chiseled angles of his cheeks and jaw.

"Being a teenage father must be a scary thing," she said, which produced another look in his eyes that made her uneasy.

"Where is he? And Holly?" he demanded.

"I don't know." That was the truth. She wouldn't know until they contacted her. "But they're together."

"I've taught him to accept the consequences of his actions. It's not like him to run away from his responsibilities,'' he said, raising his chin toward the baby in her arms.

"He didn't run away—not exactly. They just needed some space to think things through."

"They've got a little girl," he said, an edge to his voice. "What else is there to think about?"

Rachel glanced down at the sleeping baby. She lowered her own voice to just above a whisper. "Look, I'm going to put Emma down and—"

"I'll hold her."

"What?"

"Your ears tired, too?"

Now who was snapping? She wondered what his excuse was. "I heard you just fine," she said, studying him.

Why would he want to hold the baby? Weren't most men afraid to hold babies? And he was a big man— at least six feet. At her own five feet one inch, most people towered over her. But that didn't make her as cranky as Jake Fletcher towering over her. A day with a looming Jake Fletcher definitely didn't do much to sweeten her case of the tired crankies. Because he wasn't most people. He was good-looking, in a rugged, masculine way. He was a cowboy. He made her nervous.

He owned one of the biggest, most successful ranches in the Sweet Spring area. And if she was looking for signs, the black hat in his hands was a humdinger. Didn't all the bad guys wear black hats? It was almost the same color as his hair. In his dark blue eyes there was an expression of world-weary cynicism that, for reasons she didn't want to think about, chipped away at the ice surrounding her feelings about him.

Or maybe it was that darn, rather dandy dimple in

his chin. Her grandmother always said dimple on chin, devil within. Time would tell about that. But she knew he had a nice mouth—when it wasn't pinched and pressed into a line clearly indicating his irritation.

"You don't have to hold her," Rachel finally said. "I'll put her in her bassinet."

"I want to hold her. Is there some reason you don't want me to?"

Yeah, she wanted to say. Her mother doesn't trust you. Had Holly ever let him hold the baby? This infant was his niece. So unless she wanted to look like she had a heart stored in the deep freeze, she should let him. "Do you know how to hold a baby?"

"How hard can it be? She's not as heavy as a sack of oats," he said seriously.

Her eyes widened. "She's not a sack of anything. She's a baby. You know, delicate. You can't toss her around like a sack of—"

The sudden, slight upturn of his lips said "gotcha."

"Okay." Her mouth curved up reluctantly as she tucked the information away under *T* for teasing in the Jake Fletcher file. "But really, you've got to support her head."

Rachel stepped closer to him and laid the sleeping child in the crook of his arm. The fragrance of soap mingled with something—not aftershave she decided, noting stubble on his lower cheeks and jaw. He hadn't taken the time to shave, but he smelled good. She'd already noted he was a big man who dwarfed her miniscule entryway. But why did he look bigger holding a small baby? His broad shoulders seemed even broader, his thickly muscled arms stronger. Yet he held Emma as if she were priceless, breakable glass.

Rachel's insides jumped like she'd just touched a

live wire. Sleep deprivation could really do a number on your nerves, she decided.

"I'll go put on some clothes."

"Good idea," he said.

Good idea, she thought with a sigh. Second cousin to his "Good Lord" when he'd first seen her. As in she looked like road kill. Followed by, if she couldn't put a bag over her head, she should at least put some clothes on. On the bright side, clothes would make her feel less vulnerable. It was clear she needed coffee. Bad. Because under normal circumstances she wouldn't give a rat's backside what the heck Jake Fletcher thought of her.

Jake watched as Rachel disappeared through the doorway. Moments later, down the hall a door closed with just a little more force than was necessary. He made himself sit down with the baby, even though he was itching to follow Rachel and demand to know what the hell was going on. Because he had a feeling she knew more than she'd said. He badly wanted to know what Rachel Manning was hiding and why she had his brother's baby.

Glancing down at the small, warm body in his arms, Jake felt the hole he always carried inside him open wider, followed by an aching sadness. This new baby reminded him of everything that had been taken from him. But he wasn't a kid now. And it wasn't going to happen again. Not to his brother. He would see to it.

Leaning back, he snuggled Emma to his chest and glanced at the doorway where Rachel had disappeared. Her guarded expression when she'd opened the door to him said a mouthful. She'd told him once that he was butting into his brother's life, throwing his weight around. Takes one to know one. And he knew her kind—a straight-up, straight arrow, by-the-book, toe-the-line, card-carrying buttinski. She wouldn't know the meaning of minding her own business if it bit her on the fanny.

Under the circumstances he wouldn't have expected it, but that thought made him smile. Little Miss Muffet wasn't his type, thinking she knew what was best for the whole world. But she had one fine fanny. And in those pajamas that covered next to nothing, the rest of her wasn't bad, either.

The baby squirmed and squeaked and he gently settled his palm on her abdomen. It nearly covered her from chest to ankle. She was so little and the need to protect and care for her body-slammed him. This child was his niece—his family. And he was going to do right by her. This time no one would get in his way.

Almost as if Rachel had heard that thought, she came back into the room. In buttercup-yellow shorts and a matching tank top, with her golden hair mussed as if a man had run his fingers through it, she looked like a walking sunbeam. He noticed she'd washed the mascara from beneath her eyes.

She walked over to him. "I'll put Emma in her bassinet now."

She leaned over and slid her hand into the crook of his arm beneath the child's head, then nudged the other under the baby's bottom and lifted. Where Rachel's hands had touched him, a trail of warmth lingered. When her gaze locked with his, he wondered why he'd never noticed before that her eyes were so big. And brown. Normally blondes had blue eyes and the unusual coloring was nice. Almost before the thought formed, she left with the baby. Then a few moments later, she returned and closed the door that separated her living room, kitchen and dining area from what he figured were the bedrooms down the hall. She sat across from him in a green wing chair that kept the oval oak coffee table between them.

He stared at her. "Now tell me where Dan and Holly are."

Something flickered in her gaze before she said, "Like I told you before, I don't know."

A cold, hard feeling settled in his gut. "Did you know they were planning to take off?"

"Look, Jake, the kids are scared. They're trying to do the right thing—"

"Did you know?" he asked again.

"Yes, but—"

"So they ran away?"

"That implies they don't intend to come back." Her gaze met his as she let out a long breath. "They didn't run away—exactly."

"What does that mean?"

"They were making plans—find an apartment, jobs, that sort of thing. I was supposed to know where they were going. But for some reason they jumped the gun and left without telling me. At least I have something in writing from Holly giving me permission to take the baby to the doctor." The odd expression on his face made her suspicious. "Did you do something to put pressure on them? Something that made them take off?"

He shook his head. "If I'd known they were up to something— This is completely irresponsible."

"Not completely. Look at it from their point of view. They wanted time to see if they could take care of themselves."

"How much time?"

"The rest of the summer." Her hands fluttered, and she kept talking, the words tumbling out fast. "They need to think through whether or not they want to keep the baby."

"There's nothing to think about. She's Dan's responsibility." Anger surged through him and he stood, running his hand through his hair. "It's not like Dan to go off half-cocked like this. Sounds like some hare-brained scheme Holly would come up with."

Her mouth compressed to a straight line. "Actually, it was sort of my idea."

"Yours?" Jake felt as if she'd slugged him in the stomach. She was an adult who should know better. "What the hell were you thinking telling them to run off?"

"That's not exactly what I said or how it happened." She twisted her fingers together in her lap.

"I don't get it. After the baby was born, I told her the two of them could stay on the ranch. As long as she wanted."

"She wasn't comfortable with that and asked to stay with me a little longer. I agreed. There but for the grace of God and all that. She and Dan were talking about marriage. But since Emma was born, she says they've been fighting a lot. He's got a full college football scholarship."

"That I know about."

"Holly doesn't want to stand in his way. She's in a catch-22 situation. She wants to go to college, too, but she doesn't see how that can happen with taking care of Emma. On top of that, she's not even sure she and Dan will stay together. How can she do it on her own?"

"I told her I would help."

Rachel's gaze flicked to his. "She wasn't comfortable with that, either. Look, you have to understand where she's coming from. Holly loves her daughter and wants the best for her. We discussed the possibility of a stable adoptive home. If she's going to give her up—"

"Not going to happen," he said, shaking his head. "The Fletcher family takes care of its own."

"As I was saying, in the course of our talks, I casually mentioned that no one would blame her and Dan if they took time to make their decision. Because it's permanent. In fact, they have an obligation to Emma to do everything possible to determine what's best. They came up with the idea to get summer jobs and an apartment to see if they can handle it."

"Of all the irresponsible—"

"They think they *are* being responsible."

"Not them. You," he said, looking down at her.

She stood suddenly, brown eyes blazing. "How dare you judge me? You don't even know me. I agreed to care for the baby because I'd innocently said something to put the idea in their heads. And that was only after suggesting they leave the baby with you—"

He blinked. "You did?"

"Yes. But Holly adamantly refused."

"For crying out loud," he snapped. "I'm family—"

She held up her hand. "I'm just telling you what she said. Don't bite off the messenger's head. They were upset and threatened to take off. I didn't think that was a good alternative for anyone, especially the baby. And Dan said you knew and approved of the idea."

"I didn't."

"I'm only telling you what he told me."

"And you didn't think to run it by me first?" he demanded.

"He's adult enough to be a father, I figured he could make this decision on his own." She folded her arms over her chest.

"You should have figured it was a dumb thing to do and mentioned it to someone," he said.

"You mean ratted them out to you."

Jake let out a long breath as he ran his fingers through his hair again. When he got his hands on that kid—

His brother had screwed up big time. Déjà vu all over again. Was the trait wired into their DNA? He'd raised Dan after their parents died and he'd done his level best to see Dan didn't make the same mistakes Jake had. For all the good it had done. But that was a completely different issue. Jake intended to see that lightning didn't strike the Fletcher men twice.

"You might want to cut him some slack, Jake. He's got a lot to think about. So does Holly." Rachel walked to the door and opened it.

Was she throwing him out? The idea of it almost made him laugh as he looked at her five-feet-nothing, one-hundred-pounds-soaking-wet frame. What made her think he was okay with any of this and would leave? Why should he believe she didn't know where his brother was? What if she was lying? Jake had been burned in the past. He got the feeling Rachel was turning up the heat.

"I'll say one thing for you."

"What's that?" she asked.

What could it hurt to bait a hook and go on a small fishing expedition? "You're a lousy liar."

"I'm sorry you feel that way."

"So you'd rather be a good liar?" he asked, one eyebrow quirking up.

"That's not what I meant." She blew out a long breath and shook her head. "I really and truly have no idea where those kids have gone."

"Have it your way." He picked up his hat from the couch and put it on. "Makes no difference to me."

"Good."

"It doesn't change the fact that I'm taking Emma back to the ranch with me."

Chapter Two

He was taking Emma to the ranch? Over her dead body, Rachel thought. She'd wondered if this day could get any worse. Now she had her answer. Apparently the gods eagerly pounced on her negative challenge and made it so. She wanted to rephrase— could this day get any better?

Jake Fletcher *better* leave and take his sweeping pronouncements with him. She had given Holly a solemn promise to keep the child until she returned. Rachel knew how deeply a betrayal could cut. No way was this man taking Emma back to his ranch—or anywhere else for that matter.

Rachel closed her front door, then moved to block the hallway that led to the room where Emma was napping. Looking up at him, way up, she knew there was no way she could stop him if he decided to do this. But she was prepared to bluff him as best she could.

She folded her arms over her chest. "I'm not going to let you take Emma out of this apartment, Jake."

"Oh?"

"Like I told you, Holly gave her to me for safe-keeping."

"I'm not going to hurt her."

"That's your interpretation."

He shook his head. "You accused me of making judgments about you without information. Well, right back at you, Rachel. What kind of man do you think I am? I would never hurt a child, especially my own niece."

"There are lots of ways you could hurt her. Like keeping her from her mother," Rachel said.

She couldn't see his eyes because the brim of his black hat shadowed them. But Jake's mouth thinned.

"What makes you think I would do that?"

"What I think doesn't matter. It's what Holly believes. She made me promise not to give Emma to you. She thinks you're planning to take the baby away from her."

He put his hands on his hips and shook his head. "That's the last thing I'd do."

"Unfortunately I am not the person you have to convince," Rachel pointed out. "But here's the deal. I gave Holly my word that I would take care of Emma until she comes back. She made me specifically swear that I wouldn't hand the baby over to you for any reason."

"Why would she think I was planning to take Emma?" he asked.

"Because taking over is what you do, Jake."

"And how do you know this?"

"I saw it for myself. You insisted on being at the

childbirth classes. What was that about? And when Holly wouldn't follow your command to get married, you tried to talk her into going to the ranch after she left the hospital with the baby, even though she made it clear she didn't want to go anywhere with you. You questioned everything she did from the way she held the baby to how Emma was dressed. It's plain as day you don't trust her. Next you'll probably check into the electronic surveillance ankle bracelets they make prisoners wear.''

"After this stunt they've pulled, it's not a bad idea,'' he said.

"The point is, you're always there, not giving them a chance to breathe.''

"I'm supporting my brother,'' he said, an edge to his voice.

"That's commendable. But his actions speak volumes. He left with Holly. I think the two of them have had about all the support from you they can stand.''

"His actions leave a lot to be desired. He put his child in the care of an outsider,'' he said.

"An outsider maybe. But it was his decision to make, not yours,'' she pointed out. "That means I have permission from him as well as Holly to care for their baby until we have some word from them. And that's what I intend to do.''

The muscle in his lean cheek contracted. "You're interfering in a family situation.''

She chose to ignore the interfering remark. "You and Dan are family, but Holly hasn't got anyone except me.''

Rachel promised herself she would never take in another person in need. Ever. But now that she was up to her eyes in alligators on Holly's behalf, she would go to the mat on the issue of protecting Holly's rights to her baby. Mother and child went together like home and hearth.

"What if she doesn't come back?" he asked.

"Of course she'll be back," Rachel said automatically.

But she knew from firsthand experience that sometimes things happened. Sometimes mothers didn't come back. Or fathers, either. Yearning for what could never be spasmed inside her, like a hunger that could never be satisfied.

"Come on, Rachel. Be realistic. There's a story on the news almost every night about a baby abandoned, sometimes in a Dumpster."

"Holly didn't do that. She arranged for me to care for her baby until she comes back."

"*If* she comes back."

She would, Rachel thought. She was almost sure of it. "Holly didn't just run off without a word. She was breastfeeding and waited to do this as long as she could—until the baby had received the benefits of breast milk."

"If she'd stayed, Emma would still be receiving the benefits," he said.

"I'm not saying it's an ideal situation. But a lot of working mothers wean their infants because they have to return to work."

Jake folded his arms over his chest. "Sugarcoat it all you want, Rachel. She's irresponsible."

"That's your opinion."

"And I've got another one. It's weird for an attractive, single woman to turn her life upside down for a teenager's baby."

"So if I was an unattractive woman it would be

okay?'' She put her hands on her hips. "It's not like I'm going to adopt Emma. This is just for a few weeks. So unless I hear differently, I intend to keep my promise. When Holly comes back, her baby will be here waiting for her.''

Something told Rachel that Jake would be waiting, too. He was Emma's biological uncle and frustration seemed to be rolling off him in tangible waves. On the one hand, she understood Holly's concerns about Jake's tendency to take control. On the other, Rachel had to give him credit for getting involved. How many men would so aggressively seek out the burden of a newborn? She couldn't decide if he was concerned, caring or just plain crazy.

But in this regard Jake was certainly different from the men she normally met. Rachel knew her fatal flaw was her inability to turn away from someone in need. She had no illusions. No good deed went unpunished.

"So we're at an impasse,'' he said.

"Unless you decide to muscle your way past me and forcibly take Emma.''

"I'm not in the habit of manhandling women.''

A discreet look at his broad chest made her wonder what he *was* in the habit of doing with women. That thought sent an unwilling shiver over her arms.

"I'm glad to hear that,'' she said.

"Well you won't be glad to hear that I intend to stop your interference.''

"Why can't you just relax and let Holly and Dan do this their way?''

"If you would give me the baby, I'd be happy to relax. But since you refuse, I'll go to plan B.''

"That's the one where you bulldoze everyone to get

what you want.'' She nodded. ''I'll consider myself warned. And you know the way out.''

He touched the brim of his hat in what was probably an automatic, ingrained polite gesture. Then he walked out of her apartment. After turning the deadbolt and fitting the chain lock securely across the door, Rachel breathed a sigh of relief.

Jake had voiced her worst fear—what if Holly didn't come back? Rachel decided to be an optimist. No one knew better than she that the road to hell was paved with good intentions. But unless she had evidence to the contrary, she planned to keep the baby healthy and happy until she could put her back into her mother's arms.

In a perfect world, Holly and Dan would decide to get married, make a home for their baby and live happily ever after. But life wasn't a fairy tale. She shivered as the thought reminded her yet again of February 29 in New Orleans. They had joked about the scenario calling for three wishes, and they'd each had one.

If the situation she found herself in truly was a result of her birthday wish, she could only be grateful she hadn't had two more of her very own. She could be in three times as much trouble.

She tiptoed down the hall to check on the sleeping baby. Rachel smiled tenderly as she looked in the crib. Somehow, even on her back Emma had scooched her way straight up into the corner, her head butted up against the bumper pad. Touching the downy head and tiny fist with one finger, Rachel's heart contracted. Feelings as big as the wide open spaces of Texas expanded inside her.

''You're not trouble, little one,'' she whispered.

"You're nothing but a blessing. It's your uncle who's a pain in the posterior."

And not only because he was going to throw his weight around.

Three days later, Jake walked into The Fast Lane, Sweet Spring's bowling alley coffee shop, with the newspaper under his arm. He sat down in his usual booth, then stared at the tufted red Naugahyde seat across from him. It hit him suddenly that he'd never noticed the color or the tufting before. Because usually Dan sat across from him. They came here for dinner often.

Sally Jean Simmons sidled up to him, order pad and pencil in hand. "Hey, Jake. How's it goin'?"

He looked up at the tall, pretty brunette. "Okay. How about you? How's that boy of yours? He's what now? Five? Six?"

"Seven," she said smiling. "He's doin' great, thanks." She glanced at the empty seat across from him. "Where's Dan tonight?"

Jake felt the knot in his gut pull tighter. "He made other plans."

And didn't see fit to share them with me, he silently added. Every time he thought about his brother taking off without saying a word to him, he got mad all over again.

"Look on the bright side," Sally said, studying him. "Table for one will ease the strain on your wallet. The way that boy can pack away food is scary. I'm not looking forward to footin' the bills when my little guy takes a growth spurt like Dan has. What can I get you tonight?"

"Coffee for starters," he said. "And a menu."

"Since when do you need a menu?" she asked. "It hasn't changed in the five years I've been working here and you know that sucker by heart."

He shrugged. "Just thought looking at it might help me make up my mind."

"Comin' right up." Her hips swayed as she walked away.

Jake noted her curvy figure covered in tight worn denim and an equally snug T-shirt with The Fast Lane printed on the back. A vision of spiky blond hair, big brown eyes and a body dressed in sunbeam yellow flashed into his mind. It had been several days since he'd seen Rachel Manning, but she was never far from his thoughts. Partly because she was a damned attractive woman. And partly because today Little Miss Muffet was probably sorry she'd gotten between him and his family.

Behind him, the bell over the door rang as it was opened, then dinged again when it shut. He moved his napkin-wrapped eating utensils aside, then unfolded his newspaper and spread it on the Formica table in front of him. A moment later he smelled perfume and sensed someone standing beside him.

"Jake, we need to talk."

Rachel. He braced himself, but not enough. When he looked up, his gut pulled tight again, but not from anger, annoyance or regret. It was plain old-fashioned appreciation for a beautiful woman.

"Rachel," he said.

She was wearing shorts that flared a bit at her thighs and a tank top made out of T-shirt material with skinny straps that curved over her tanned shoulders. Her hair was combed this time in a deliberately mussed style that looked like a man had just run his fingers through it. The circles beneath her eyes were deeper and darker than they'd been a few days before. That awareness stirred the annoying protective streak he'd first noticed that morning in her apartment. Hardening himself against the feeling, he turned his attention to the baby carrier she held. Emma was supposed to be the primary focus of this newly discovered protective streak.

"Have a seat," he said, indicating the place across from him.

"This isn't a social call."

"Didn't think it was, but you can still sit."

She shifted the carrier to her other hand, then flexed her fingers as if the combined weight of Emma and the contraption had taken a toll. He reached over and took the infant seat from her, then set it on the table.

His heart contracted at the sight of the sleeping baby. Her little mouth was puckered up and moving as if she sucked an imaginary bottle in her sleep. Long, dark lashes curved above cheeks just beginning to show signs of getting chubby. Jake didn't know the first thing about babies, but this one was a stunner in his book.

"How's she doin'?"

"Great."

It was just one word, but there was a softness in Rachel's voice that made him look up. Her expression as she stared at the baby held a tenderness he wouldn't have expected from a woman so tenacious and hardheaded.

"Everything all right?" he asked, glancing at the little girl sleeping in the seat.

"She's perfect," Rachel answered, placing a hand on the carrier.

Just then Sally Jean returned. "Here you go, Jake. Coffee and a menu." She glanced at Rachel. "Need another one?"

"No," Rachel said.

"Yes," he answered at the same time.

"I'm not staying for dinner."

"Have you already eaten?" he asked.

"No, but that's not why I'm—"

"On second thought," he told Sally Jean. "We'll have two orders of meatloaf, mashed potatoes and gravy."

"I'm not hungry," Rachel said.

"It comes with a salad or soup," Sally Jean said.

Jake studied Rachel and figured she was a greens kind of gal. "We'll have salad with thousand island dressing."

"Biscuits, French rolls, or garlic toast?"

"Garlic toast," he answered, deciding there was no way the two of them would be kissing.

"Comin' right up," the waitress said, then moved away.

"I came to talk to you, not to eat dinner," Rachel informed him.

"You can kill two birds." And in that vein, he figured buying her dinner could feather his own nest. If he was nice to her, maybe he could soften her up and talk her into bowing out gracefully.

Rachel stared at him and before she could respond, two old ladies, one with gray hair, the other bright red, slid out of the booth behind her. Jake spent a lot of time on the ranch and didn't recognize the two women. When they started past, Gray Hair stopped by Emma's car seat and peeked in.

"Congratulations," she said, looking from Rachel to him. "What a beautiful baby."

"Isn't she?" Rachel said to them. "Cora Edens, Janie Compton, I'd like you to meet Jake Fletcher."

"Hello," gray-haired Cora said.

"Nice to meet you." Flame-haired Janie stuck out her hand and Jake shook it.

"Rachel, dear," Cora said. "I didn't know you were married."

"Oh, it's not what—"

"Or pregnant," Janie said, looking at the baby. "What's her name?"

"Emma," Rachel answered.

"She's a beauty." Cora glanced at Jake. "She's got the same indentation in her chin as her father. I think she'll have your coloring, too. Can't tell much from that fuzz all over her head, but my guess is her hair will be dark."

"Yes, ma'am," he answered, unsure what response to make, but knowing one was required. He could have said they weren't married and Emma wasn't theirs, but that was a can of worms he didn't particularly want to open.

"Cora, Janie," Rachel said, "Jake and I aren't married. This isn't what you think—"

Apparently Rachel didn't feel the same way about worms.

Janie put a finger to her lips. "Don't you fret. Far be it from me to judge you and your young man for doing the wild thing."

"No, it's not that—"

"If I was a few years younger, I'd be suckered by those blue eyes, too, honey. I just know you and your fella will do right by this baby and get married. It's plain as day.'' Cora patted her arm, then took another look into the carrier. "She's somethin'.''

Janie curved her fingers around the other woman's arm. "C'mon, sister. We have to go before you embarrass this nice young couple any more. Good to see you, Rachel. Jake, nice to meet you.''

"Wait—'' Rachel held her hand up as the bell above the door double-dinged their departure. She met his gaze and there was a hint of a grin in her brown eyes. "Why didn't you set them straight?''

"Because I saw how you were wasting your breath,'' he said. "Besides, I was too busy trying to wrap my mind around that 'wild thing' remark.''

"I'm sorry,'' she said, her cheeks pink. "I had no idea talking to you here would be a problem.''

"No harm done.''

"That may not be entirely true.''

"How do you know those two? Doesn't seem like you'd travel in the same circles.''

"Cora was in the hospital when she broke her hip and had surgery. As soon as a patient is admitted, it's my job to juggle their course of treatment with their insurance reimbursement. I also check into nursing homes and rehabilitation facilities. In Cora's case, she needed heavy-duty physical therapy to get her back on her feet. It's nice to see her up and around. On the other hand, she's up and around and moving so well the whole town will think we've had a baby together.''

"Are you saying that sweet little old lady has a big mouth?''

"Mouths. Plural. Those two sweet little old ladies spread stories like a farmer spreads manure,'' she said, sitting down across from him.

Jake laughed. He couldn't help himself. Then Sally

Jean set two salads in front of them. With her hands on her hips, she looked from Rachel to Jake. "You two look like you're havin' fun."

Jake wouldn't go that far. But if anyone had told him he would be laughing over dinner with the woman who was messing with his family, he'd have called the person crazy.

"Entrées will be out in a few," she said, and walked away without waiting for an answer.

"Eat. You need to keep your strength up." But when the smile disappeared from Rachel's face, part of him wanted to call the words back.

"My strength? Because of the baby," she guessed, her gaze narrowed on him. "If you have your way, that won't be an issue much longer."

"You got the papers?" he asked.

"Regarding Emma's custody hearing? Yes," she said, picking up her fork.

Jake studied her, wondering if she was planning to stab him with it. Just a moment before, when she'd laughed with him, her brown eyes had been sweet and warm as cocoa. Now her expression was pinched and uncomfortable, as if her panties had shrunk two sizes.

"How could you, Jake?"

"You left me no choice."

"There's always a choice. I'm here to try to talk you into dropping your custody petition."

"Now why would I do that after that high-priced attorney spent so much time on it?"

"Because you want what's best for Emma."

He didn't see it that way. But the least he could do was hear her out. "Tell me how ignoring the fact that my niece isn't with her family is in her best interest."

"You don't have to ignore anything—especially

her. In fact I would encourage you to spend as much time with Emma as you'd like. Keeping this situation out of the court system is what would be best for everyone. It's not too late to rescind the paperwork.''

"I can't do that.''

"Jake, listen to me," she pleaded. "You must see that ideally Emma should be with Holly and Dan. They're her parents.''

"Okay. I'll grant you that." He met her gaze. "But they're not here at the moment. They took off and left their child with you. I don't see that as ideal.''

"Me, neither. But where's the harm in leaving things status quo?''

"I'm just making sure my brother's rights are protected.''

"I'm not going to trample his rights. I'd like nothing more than to put this child in his arms and Holly's. That's what I plan to do as soon as possible. But if the court gets involved, it will only complicate issues when Holly and Dan come back.''

"How can you be so sure about Holly?'' he asked.

For an instant doubt shadowed her eyes, making them dark and distant. A moment later the look disappeared. Determination hardened her expression, compressing her full lips.

"I told you before, Jake, this is her baby. She'll be back." Rachel sat up straighter and met his gaze. "For that matter, what about your brother?''

"What about him?''

"You keep doubting Holly, but what about Dan?''

"Say it straight out, Rachel.''

"He lied to me," she reminded him. "How do you know he won't keep on running?''

If he knew what was good for him he would, Jake

thought, trying to decide what sort of punishment would fit this crime. But sooner or later the Fletcher instincts would kick in. Dan would do the right thing.

"He belongs here. The land is in his blood. He'll be back," Jake said, absolutely convinced he spoke the truth.

"Then there's no reason to go to court. Emma will be fine with me until her parents come home."

It wasn't that simple. He'd had a child taken from him; he knew how it felt. He wouldn't stand by and do nothing while the same thing happened to his brother. This time he wasn't a boy. No one was going to take advantage of him.

"It's nothing personal, Rachel."

"Then why does it feel that way?"

"I couldn't say. I've learned not to take chances. Do unto others before they do it to me."

"That's awfully cynical."

"I've got my reasons."

"Of course." She put her fork down, leaving the salad untouched. "But I'm wondering if I should be insulted."

"That wasn't my intention. I'm just trying to protect Dan."

"I assure you that I have no intention of hurting him. I'm just trying to keep you from inadvertently hurting Holly."

"I have nothing against Holly."

"Then I propose we try to find the kids and talk the whole thing over."

"I've got a private investigator looking for them. In the meantime, we'll talk it over in court and let a judge make the decision."

Rachel shook her head. "If this gets into the judicial system, it's out of our hands. Don't you see, Jake?"

"Yeah, I see fine."

"But you won't change your mind?"

"Not a chance. Not when I'm holding all the cards."

She slid out of the booth and picked up the infant carrier. "I guess I'll see you in court."

Then she was gone and the bell over the door double-dinged. He stared again at the tufted red Naugahyde across from him. The Fast Lane felt suddenly empty. What was that all about? An evening that had stretched out before him pretty dreary and depressing had picked up considerably when Rachel had arrived. Now she was gone and he was alone. Again.

Jake found he was looking forward to seeing her in court—for all the wrong reasons.

Chapter Three

After parking in the designated area at the court-house, Rachel got out, opened the rear door of her compact car and released the restraints on Emma's carrier. The baby was sleeping soundly, lulled by the car's motion on the short ride from the apartment to the square in the center of downtown Sweet Spring.

Sighing, Rachel thought how beautiful this child was with her full cheeks, soft skin and cupid's bow mouth. Sometimes her feelings were so big she was overwhelmed and reminded herself to keep her emotions in check. But how did one censor such a thing? It was there every time she looked at Emma, got bigger when she picked the baby up and held her, fed, bathed and rocked her to sleep.

She'd wondered whether or not to bring the baby to the legal proceeding. In the event the ruling went against her and it was necessary to surrender the baby, she'd decided to bring Emma along. Rachel's legal counsel was the hospital's attorney who assessed risk management at the medical facility and had volunteered her time as a favor. Although child custody wasn't her sphere of expertise, the lawyer had done some research. She'd cautioned that in these cases, nothing was cut-and-dried and there were no guarantees.

Rachel had mixed feelings. Part of her wished Jake would win and it would be over. She stared at the baby as she lifted the carrier out of the car and her heart gave a funny little lurch, as if the earth tilted. Then she thought of Holly whose maternal feelings must be ten times as strong. Rachel knew she had to do everything possible to protect the teenager's rights. Who else did Holly have in her corner?

But every time Rachel championed someone in need, she got ripped off—either her money or her heart. She brushed a finger across Emma's cheek and realized this time she could lose both.

Crossing the blacktop parking area, she noticed a truck pull into the lot and recognized Jake behind the wheel. She hadn't seen him for almost a week. Before things had turned adversarial between them that night in The Fast Lane, she'd enjoyed talking and laughing with him. She'd thought about that often in the days since. He had a nice smile and the crinkle lines around his blue eyes indicated he did it often. Just not with her.

But the tender way he'd looked at Emma… Well, Rachel's heart had come dangerously close to a meltdown. It was the way she'd always imagined a parent looking at a child—the way her father and mother would have looked at her. If they'd lived.

Wow, what was it about this situation that was stirring up all her most painful memories?

Jake started toward the courthouse, then hesitated when he saw her. He was wearing a navy suit and red tie. His thick dark hair was conservatively cut and neatly combed and she couldn't help thinking he cleaned up pretty nice. But there was something about the bad boy black cowboy hat and the way he filled out his jeans—it was silly, maybe even stupid, but she missed that impossibly male look.

He walked over to her. "Hello, Rachel."

"Jake."

His gaze slid to the baby carrier. "How's Emma?"

"Sleeping like a baby." She had the satisfaction of seeing his mouth quirk up.

"Is it my imagination, or is she bigger than the last time I saw her?"

"No, you're not imagining it." Rachel shifted the carrier to her other hand. "It's almost as if I can *see* her growing."

"Can I take her for you?" He reached out, his big hand strong and steady.

She hesitated for just a moment. Would it violate the promise she'd made to Holly? Heck, she'd already let him hold the baby. But they were on opposite sides of this issue and she probably shouldn't even be talking to him. Still, Emma was his niece. It would be more wrong to be inflexible.

She handed the baby over. "Thanks."

"Don't mention it."

He automatically took her elbow as they crossed the blacktop then climbed the steps to the imposing stone courthouse. It was the legal hub of the city and a busy place. People milled around talking or hurried in and out of the building. Many of them glanced in the infant carrier and smiled at the sleeping baby, then nodded at her and Jake. After Cora and Janie made their assumption that night at The Fast Lane, Rachel figured anyone who looked would also assume they were a couple and Emma belonged to the two of them. Soon the baby would be with one of them legally, if only temporarily. Unless… Rachel decided to try one more time to talk him into dropping his petition.

She put a restraining hand on his arm when he reached out to open the glass door to the building. "Can I talk to you for a minute—before we go in?"

"Okay. What?"

She looked up at him and smiled. "This is way too civilized for two people who are going to do battle shortly."

"I heard you hired an attorney."

"I have legal counsel. Whatever happens, I figured I'd give it my best shot for Holly's sake." If she'd been with her own mother while she'd been growing up, Rachel wondered if she would be going to the mat on this. Between that tragedy and her unfortunate, yet inherent nature to champion the underdog, she decided she had no choice.

She looked up at him and put her hand up to shield her eyes from the sun's glare. "I've been thinking about what you said the other night."

"What did I say?" he asked, frowning.

"Do unto others before they can do it to you. I just wanted to make sure you understand that I'm not trying to do *anything* to you. I'm just keeping a promise to a young girl who has to live for the rest of her life with the decision she makes. In that spirit, won't you consider skipping the legal stuff? Can't we take care of Emma together until the kids come back?"

He let out a long breath. "Look, Rachel, Holly

might be okay with you running things, but I'm not. Emma is Dan's child, too—and my family. No one goes through life without baggage, including me. But you're interfering in a family matter.''

''I'm just trying to be the voice of reason and minimize Emma's baggage to a small carry-on. By making sure she's reunited with her mother.''

''Fathers have rights, too, and I won't stand by and do nothing while my brother's are ignored.''

She decided it was best not to point out that Dan had exercised his paternal rights when the teens had made the decision to leave the baby in her care.

Before she had a chance to form a logical response to his comment, her attorney walked up the courthouse steps. She glanced warily at Jake, then joined them.

''Are you ready?'' she asked Rachel.

''Yes. Kara Swanson this is Jake Fletcher. Kara's my attorney.''

Kara nodded. ''Mr. Fletcher.''

''Miss Swanson.'' His eyes narrowed.

''I'll take Emma now, Jake,'' she said, holding out her hand for the carrier.

His expression said he would rather chew rusty nails than hand her over. But he only hesitated a moment before letting her take the infant. ''See you in court.''

After one final glance, he disappeared through the glass doors into the building. Rachel, with her attorney beside her, followed him. Their shoes echoed on the wooden floor as they looked for the right courtroom. When it was located, they went through two heavy mahogany doors. There was an aisle between rows of wooden seats and Rachel couldn't help feeling it was an awful lot like church. But she'd been to church; she'd never been in a courtroom before and found it pretty intimidating. She followed Kara to the front of the room, then set the baby on a table that faced the judge's bench.

On the other side of the aisle, Jake conferred in muted whispers with his white-haired attorney. Rachel recognized the man was Walter Allen. Kara had told her he had a reputation for winning. She'd also said she'd filed a legal brief on Rachel's behalf. The judge would read it along with Jake's, then render a decision on the petition. The next thing Rachel knew, a black-robed woman marched into the room followed by a bailiff dressed in the khaki uniform of the sheriff's department.

"All rise for Judge Olivia Edwards."

They stood and faced the attractive brunette who looked to be in her late forties. After settling behind the bench, the judge put on her glasses and stared at everyone assembled.

"You may be seated," she said, then looked at the other table. "How are you, Jake?"

"Fine, Olivia," he answered.

"It's 'Your Honor' while I'm wearing this robe," she chided with a smile.

Rachel looked from him to the judge. They were on a first name basis? So when he'd said he was holding all the cards, that probably meant he had a friend or at the very least an acquaintance on the bench. So much for the scales of justice being balanced.

"Your Honor—" Jake's attorney stayed standing.

"Mr. Allen," the judge said.

"It would be a mistake to minimize the importance of this baby living with Mr. Fletcher. He's her uncle, a blood relative who—"

Kara jumped to her feet. "Objection, Your Honor.

Genes and DNA don't give him qualifications or credentials to care for an infant. He's not married and has no children of his own—"

"Miss Manning is also single and has never been a mother," Walter countered.

Kara glanced from him to the judge. "She's a woman—"

"Being of the female gender doesn't make her any more qualified than Mr. Fletcher, Your Honor."

"We're willing to concede to an even playing field," Kara said.

"It's not even. That's what we're arguing," the other attorney said. "As the child's uncle, Mr. Fletcher has the greater claim."

"But, Mr. Fletcher's own brother—"

"Enough," the judge said, glancing from one to the other. "All of this is in the briefs. I want to hear from each petitioner in their own words. You first, Miss Manning. You're not a relative of the child in question?"

Rachel stood. "No, Your Honor. I'm a friend of Holly Johnson, the baby's mother."

"According to Mr. Fletcher, she's abandoned her child."

"That's not true. She's coming back," Rachel said.

"You can't know that for sure." The judge studied her. "She's an acquaintance. So why are you going above and beyond the call of duty to keep this baby?"

How did she put her feelings into words, Rachel wondered. "Not *keep* the baby, Your Honor, it's temporary."

The judge nodded. "I see."

"Holly and Dan are smart enough to know they

have to be able to take care of themselves first before they can raise their baby. They asked me to care for Emma while they found an apartment and jobs—to see if they can support themselves. Just for the summer.''

''And you agreed?''

''Yes.''

''Even though this plan is irresponsible at best?'' the judge asked.

''Yes.''

''I don't understand why you would go out on a limb like this for a teenager you've only known a short time,'' the judge said.

''Your Honor, there are stories in the news every day about someone sitting in a hundred year old tree to keep it from being cut down. Or a small rowboat sitting between fishermen and the gray whale they're about to slaughter. Usually people like this are labeled bleeding heart liberals. I guess I'm hardwired to be one of them and champion the underdog. My friends keep telling me I've got to stop being taken in by sob stories and sad eyes.'' She took a deep breath. ''And I will. As soon as Emma is settled and secure. Because that's just it, Your Honor. We're not talking about a tree or a whale. We're here because of a baby. And I believe strongly that a mother's bond with her child shouldn't be challenged without a really good reason. This mother is asking for some time. While she takes it, I'm here to make sure her rights are protected. That's why I'm going out on a limb. Just until Holly and Dan return. That's it, Your Honor.''

''What do you have to say about this, Mr. Fletcher?'' the judge asked.

Jake stood. ''I offered to help Dan financially,

Olivia—I mean, Your Honor. I suggested they live at the ranch.''

"Holly was afraid Jake would take her baby if she agreed to live under his roof while he supported them,'' Rachel said.

"I see here,'' the judge said, glancing at something in front of her, ''that the baby's mother is adamantly opposed to the child being placed with you, Jake.''

"Your Honor,'' he said wryly, ''you know good and well the baby's father is my brother. That baby is family and belongs with me while I try to locate Dan. Until then, I'm going to make sure *his* rights are protected. And that's all I have to say,'' he finished, glancing at Rachel.

"It seems your brother was involved in the decision to leave the child with Miss Manning.'' The judge removed her glasses. ''So what we've got here are two people protecting the rights of teenagers who abandoned this child.''

"They're coming back,'' Rachel interjected quickly.

"Time will tell.'' The judge looked from one to the other. ''Very often in a situation like this the child is placed in foster care while these things are sorted out. But I'm not going to do that.''

"Thanks, Your Honor,'' Jake said. ''I appreciate—''

"Not so fast,'' she said. ''By all accounts you and Miss Manning are upstanding individuals. Both of you are determined to take care of this baby as well as protect the parental rights of each respective teen. And it seems absurd to place her in an already overburdened foster care system.'' She looked at each of them. ''It's my belief that you should share joint *temporary* custody of this minor infant.''

"Wait just a minute, Olivia," Jake said. "We've been friends for a long time."

"Is that so?" Rachel met his gaze. "And yet the scales of justice equaled out. So much for holding all the cards."

He glared at the judge. "You mean to tell me I can't take my niece home?"

"You need to work that out with Miss Manning." She looked down at the paperwork in front of her. "We'll revisit this issue at the end of the summer when the teens in question are finished with their social science experiment. They'd better be here or all the good intentions in the world won't protect their rights."

Jake knocked on Rachel's apartment door and waited. He knew she was there; he'd followed her from the courthouse. Every time he thought about the judge's decision he got mad all over again—if he'd ever cooled off at all. What had made him think things would go his way this time? Because his friend, the judge, was hearing the case. Some friend she'd turned out to be. At least it hadn't gone completely against him. That was something.

But they were right back where they'd started from—taking care of the baby together. As if that wasn't bad enough, it was legally mandated. If she didn't have his niece, no way would he be here, giving her the opportunity to say I told you so.

He heard footsteps, then the click of the lock. The door opened and there she was. "Hi, Jake. I thought that was you following me."

"You won this round."

"In spite of the fact that you knew a friend of yours

was going to hear the case. Anyway, does there have to be a winner?'' Rachel looked up at him with big, brown innocent eyes. ''I'd say it was a tie.''

''Call it what you want. The fact is, like it or not, we're stuck with each other. We need to talk about how this joint custody thing is going to work.''

''Come in,'' she said, stepping back to admit him. ''I agree we need to establish ground rules.''

He'd like to make ground rule number one that she tone down her sex appeal. The first time he'd dropped by her apartment, he'd been very aware of her feminine charms. Every time he'd seen her since, the feeling intensified. It didn't help that today she was wearing a figure-hugging sleeveless denim dress that stopped at her knees. From there down he couldn't ignore her shapely legs and trim ankles. He knew she'd worn shoes in court, but she didn't have them on now and for some reason the sight of her bare feet and red-painted toenails pumped up his response to her. He'd have to learn to ignore the feelings.

''Thanks,'' he said, moving past her. ''It's hot out here.''

The fragrance of flowers drifted in the air around her and he toyed with the idea of adding another ground rule: no provocative perfume.

''Okay,'' she said after closing the door. She faced him in her living room, crossing her arms over her breasts. ''How do you think we should handle this?''

''Bring Emma to the ranch.''

Just then there was a loud wail from down the hall. Rachel started toward the doorway, then glared at him over her shoulder. ''No way.''

There was another infant cry, louder this time. ''Is she all right?'' he asked, concerned.

"She just woke up. It's time for her to eat." She pointed to a microwave. "I just warmed a bottle for her."

Jake followed her down the hall and into the spare room where Emma slept in her car seat.

"I left her in here so she could finish her nap," she said, bending over to lift the whimpering baby.

He'd already acknowledged that Rachel had a fine fanny, but that was before he'd seen it with denim pulled tight across her curves. Her backside should be declared a national treasure or a lethal weapon. He wasn't sure which.

When she finished changing Emma's diaper, she scooped her up and headed into the kitchen. After grabbing the bottle, she sat on the couch and stuck the rubber nipple into the whimpering infant's mouth. Instant silence, followed by an eager, noisy smacking sound. His niece was one hungry little girl, he thought, sitting in the wing chair across from them. He wasn't sure why that should make him proud, but it did.

Rachel met his gaze. "Okay, while we have some quiet we can discuss how to handle this."

"The ranch is where she belongs. Besides, the house is bigger than your apartment."

"But you live way the heck in the middle of nowhere. My job is at the hospital here in town. It's closer for me if I stay here. The problem is I work three, twelve-hour shifts. It's considered full time and pretty intense when I do it. I'd rather not have to drive all the way out to your place when my day is over."

"You can't take her with you to work," he pointed out.

"I wasn't planning to."

"So who's going to watch Emma?"

"I was going to ask my grandmother. She loves babies. And she raised me," she added, as if that were the deciding piece of information for a child care résumé. "And, in my opinion, did a fine job."

"I've got a ranch to run," he said.

"No one is stopping you from doing that."

"I don't put in three shifts a week. It's twenty-four/seven. If you stayed at the ranch your drive to work would be a little longer, but—"

"You wouldn't be inconvenienced," she guessed. Before he could answer she said, "While you're working nonstop, who's going to watch Emma?"

He ran his fingers through his hair. "I've got ranch hands—"

"To take care of a baby?" she cried. "Just strap her to the saddle and head out to the range?"

"Of course not." He hadn't quite thought this through, but she wasn't helping with her cross-examination. "I'll delegate the work, and *I'll* watch Emma when you're at the hospital."

Rachel shook her head. "I've always heard possession is nine-tenths of the law. That's why you want her there."

"Look, when couples split up and have joint custody, don't they usually take the kids a week at a time and alternate weekends? We could do that."

"I don't like it. Emma's too little to be bounced back and forth like a ping pong ball."

"How about she stays here with you while you're not working and stays on the ranch with me when you are."

"I don't like the idea of being away from her."

"Neither do I," he said.

"And I don't like the thought of driving back and

forth while I'm working. And I still have to check with my grandmother about watching Emma.''

''I'll do it,'' he said.

''Ask my grandmother?''

''No.'' He didn't like the fact that he'd caught himself starting to smile. ''I'll take care of her while you're at work.''

''Don't you have a ranch to run?''

''I can work it out.''

''Now you can work it out? What happened to chores twenty-four/seven?''

''I'm learning to compromise.'' He met her gaze. ''But here's the deal. We have to share custody. I think you're right about spending time with the baby while she's getting to know us. I'll watch her here when you put in your shifts at the hospital.''

''You'd come here to watch Emma?'' she asked warily, as if she expected him to take exception to her statement.

''Yes. But turnabout is fair play,'' he said.

''What does that mean?''

''When you're not working, Emma comes to the ranch.''

''Holly didn't want me to hand the baby over to you.''

''You wouldn't be doing that—if you stayed with her.''

She was quiet for several moments as she watched the baby taking her bottle. Then Rachel met his gaze. ''I have a bad feeling you just suggested a perfectly reasonable compromise. I wish I could find a flaw in it, but I can't.'' Tipping her head to the side, she studied him. ''I also can't tell whether or not you'd be happy about it.''

"It doesn't matter. I don't have a choice."

"That's not true. You could walk away and let me deal with this baby all by myself."

"You'd like that wouldn't you?" He stared at her, but before she responded, he said, "Backing off is not an option."

"You don't happen to like it, but it certainly is an option. Since you're choosing to be a part of Emma's life, I have two things to say."

"Such as?"

"First, you need to loosen up. You're strung so tight you're about to snap. Just an observation, mind you. But Emma will sense it. Second, you're allowed to be crabby for a specified amount of time, then get over it."

He blinked at her bluntness. "Get over it?"

"Yes. I'm not saying you need to do the happy dance or anything. But we're stuck with each other. It would be more pleasant if you didn't scowl at me the entire time."

Was he scowling? More important—did she really think it was that easy to just let it go? He watched her watching the baby in her arms who was working for all she was worth at sucking down her formula. Suddenly, Emma squirmed and fussed and waved her arms and legs.

Rachel removed the bottle. "Do you have a bubble in your tummy, little girl?" she crooned to the baby.

Supporting Emma's head, she lifted the infant to her diaper-draped shoulder as if it were the easiest thing in the world. The last time he'd held the baby, Jake remembered being grateful she'd been content where she was and he hadn't had to move her. Rachel patted the tiny back, then slid her palm up, gently pressing as she did. She was rewarded with a very unlady-like burp.

He grinned in spite of the irritation he'd felt only moments ago. "If baby burping were an Olympic event, she'd take the gold. She's a Fletcher all right."

"I can't believe that's a family trait one would take pride in." Rachel met his gaze and tried to look stern.

She failed. The twinkle in her brown eyes was a dead giveaway. His gut tensed at the look and that didn't make him especially happy. Not only that, he envied the way she was completely comfortable with the baby, which didn't sweeten his temper, either.

Jake hadn't thought past the fact that he wanted Emma under his roof. But he could see that when she got there, she would need tending. And he didn't know the first thing about caring for an infant. His own mother had stolen that from him.

But that was a hill he'd died on a long time ago. Right now he had more important things to deal with than a past he couldn't change. He needed to make sure he and Rachel understood each other and this damn compromise.

Rachel wouldn't go to the ranch full time, so he would have to go to her. And he wasn't about to let his niece out of his sight. "Okay, so this is what we're doing. When you're working your three days, I'll come and watch Emma. The other four days, you bring her to the ranch."

Rachel nodded. "But can you be spared? I mean you said the workload—"

"My foreman can pick up the slack. Three days straight without me there isn't that long—"

"Whoa, cowboy. Why wouldn't you be there for three full days?"

"Because I'll be here."

"You're talking about being here the whole time? Like seventy-two hours without going home?"

"If you're asking will I be sleeping here, the answer is yes. Then I'll return the favor when you come out to the ranch for four days. You'll be comfortable there."

"I'm not sure you'll be very comfortable here. I'm not really equipped for overnight guests."

"Where did Holly sleep?"

"I have a futon in what used to be my computer room. But—"

"That'll do."

"It's kind of hard and uncomfortable."

There was a lot of that going around, he thought, shifting in his seat. "No big deal. I've bunked down on the ground a time or two."

"But it's sort of small for a big man like you—" She let out a long breath. "Your feet are going to hang off."

"I'll survive."

Clouds covered Rachel's sunny look and didn't show signs of lifting any time soon. "You're sure you don't want me to ask my grandmother?"

He settled his booted ankle on the opposite knee. "If I didn't know better, I'd say you were trying to get around the judge's ruling about sharing custody."

"Nothing could be further from the truth."

"Then let me worry about whether or not I'm comfortable during my shift with Emma."

"Okay. But don't say I didn't warn you."

Chapter Four

After her twelve-hour shift, Rachel parked in her car port then headed to her apartment. Looking around, she didn't see Jake's truck in the visitor area. A knot of anxiety tightened in her abdomen as she tried unsuccessfully to remember if she'd noticed it when she'd left for work.

He'd shown up bright and early that morning with a small duffel bag. She'd written down everything she could think of that he might need to know to care for Emma, then gave him a verbal rundown of her routine. She'd shown him the list of phone numbers he might need, including her work and cell and her grandmother's. Leaving him with Holly's baby had gone against every instinct she had, but there was that unfortunate "joint" in the custody ruling. That meant they had to share. Play nice. It's a good thing the judge hadn't said trust each other. Because right now she would be in contempt of court.

Would Jake take the baby back to the ranch even

after they'd agreed to this compromise? At the very least, that would be a violation of the spirit of the judge's order. But Rachel was well aware it's what he wanted. It had been his very first suggestion in their negotiation.

She'd called a few times during the day, and he'd always picked up. Except for the last time. So it had been several hours since she'd last talked to him—plenty of time to take off with Emma.

Rachel hurried to unlock her door and go inside. When she saw Jake on the sofa with Emma, relief took the starch out of her and she let out a long breath. After setting down her purse, she realized he hadn't said anything and she moved farther into the room where the dim light illuminated the scene.

Jake was semi-reclined on the sofa with his long legs stretched out in front of him, feet resting on the coffee table. He'd removed his boots and there was something so masculine yet down-to-earth about his sturdy white socks. His eyes were closed. Emma was curled up on his chest, her tiny tushy sticking in the air, his big hand resting protectively on her back. How cute was this? Rachel swallowed the lump of emotion in her throat.

With her misgivings eased, she looked around the room. Parts of different infant outfits and disposable diapers littered the floor. Several baby bottles, remnants of formula in the bottom, rested on the end tables. A couple of receiving blankets and a pacifier or two were scattered over the remaining flat surfaces. Disaster area was an understatement.

"Hi."

The rusty, deep voice raised goose bumps that scattered up and down her arms.

"Hi, yourself," she said, noticing he'd opened one eye.

He cleared his throat. "As you can plainly see I've got everything under control."

"And did you manage this control before or after the tornado came through?"

"If you'd come in a couple minutes later, I'd have had time to straighten up."

"I see. So this disaster is my fault for being prompt."

"I'm glad you grasp the finer points of the situation so quickly." His voice was a low, deep rumble just above a whisper. "Seriously though, there were a couple times I was afraid I'd gotten in over my head."

"Just a couple?"

"Yeah. It's not as easy as I thought it would be. She wore me out."

The sound of his voice sent heat to mix with the goose bumps doing the wave over her arms. "And vice versa. You finally got her to sleep and didn't want to move," she guessed, studying the way he was sprawled on her sofa.

"Right in one," he confirmed.

"And before this happened, did she have a bath?"

"That depends on how you define bath."

"I define it as a general immersion in water followed by a shampoo, body sudsing and good rinse. How do you define it?"

"General rubdown." He met her gaze. "It's good enough for the horses."

"I'm guessing the whole infant body immersion thing spooked you?"

"Define spooked." His eyes narrowed. "On second thought, never mind."

"Tell me water was used in some form during this rubdown."

"It was."

"Then I guess she'll survive. Because she's sleeping so nicely, I hate to rouse her." She lifted her chin toward the infant curled on his chest. "Can I help you out there, big guy?"

"What did you have in mind?"

"I'll put her in her bed."

"Can you do that? Without waking her?"

"I'll give it my best shot."

"Okay. But if it all goes to hell, you get to put her to sleep again."

"Understood." Rachel moved forward and stared down at him.

His gaze met hers and there was a flicker of something in his face—a potent intensity that made her shiver. Her feminine awareness of this very masculine cowboy was a bad, bad thing. It gave him an edge. At worst, she could make a fool of herself and wouldn't that complicate the heck out of their tenuous truce. Somehow, she had to figure out how to neutralize her reaction. And fast.

"What are you waiting for?" he asked, wincing when he shifted, as if his muscles were stiff and uncomfortable.

"I'm scoping this out and trying to devise my strategy."

Translation: how was she going to lift Emma without touching Jake? He was sexy as all get out, with his five-o'clock shadow and the smoky expression in his eyes. What female wouldn't feel secure in his arms? So much for dialing down her reaction.

"No pressure, Rachel, but my back is killing me," he said. "I have to stretch."

"I'm working on it." Did her voice sound as breathy as she thought?

Surely it was nothing more than a response to the physical attributes of a good looking man, a strong man capable of protecting his own. It was a trait many women found appealing. But Rachel didn't trust feelings. She'd done that too many times. From painful experience she'd learned not to let her guard down and risk getting ripped off.

If it was only her, she might have been tempted to overlook the past and let her guard down one more time—just to explore her fascination. But Emma had been entrusted to her. She had an obligation to keep a clear head, to see that Jake didn't get to her and take advantage. She had to remain objective and vigilant. She had to pick up this baby, and there was no way to do it without touching him.

"No offense," he said, "but the Allies didn't take this long to plan the invasion of Europe."

"Okay. Here goes."

Steeling herself, Rachel leaned forward and rolled Emma to the side, then cradled her head and slid a hand beneath the baby's rump. Rachel did it fast. Not only to minimize the disturbance to the baby, but to minimize her exposure to Jake. When something was hot, prolonged contact was just plain dumb.

Emma squeaked and squirmed as Rachel walked down the hall with her. In the bedroom, she put the baby on her back in the crib and waited several moments. When Emma settled herself without waking, Rachel tiptoed out of the room and pulled the door half closed.

She went back to the living room and caught her breath as she saw Jake from the rear, stretching his arms out in front of him. Obviously his muscles had become cramped from too long in one position. She noted, not for the first time, that he had some seriously fine muscles, from his neck and shoulders all the way down to his backside. The denim of his jeans was soft and worn, the material nearly white. The fabric molded like a second skin to the thick muscles in his thighs. The sight of such a fine specimen of a man made her mouth go dry.

This was a dandy time to remember that he was spending the night under her roof. And two more nights after that. She'd warned him he probably wouldn't be comfortable. No one had warned her she wouldn't be comfortable, either, for completely different reasons.

"Mission accomplished," she said.

He turned and listened. "Hear that?"

"What? Is it Emma?" she asked, straining to hear the slightest sound from the baby.

He shook his head. "Listen."

"What?"

"Silence."

Before she could respond, there was a knock on the door, startling her. "I wonder who could that be."

"I'll get it."

When he opened the door, she saw a guy standing outside with a large, flat box. "Pizza delivery," he said.

She moved next to Jake. "We didn't order anything."

He looked down at her. "I did. Thought you'd be tired and hungry when you got home. My expertise begins and ends with grilling meat on the barbecue. Since that wasn't happening, I figured pizza and salad would hit the spot. I managed to get a call out in one of Emma's quiet moments.''

"Good idea. I'll get my purse," she said, starting to turn away.

"It's taken care of."

"Tip?"

"That, too," he said, taking the box and another bag from the teenaged delivery boy. "Thanks."

"Anytime."

After the door was closed, she went into the kitchen and pulled a couple of plates from the cupboard and set them at a right angle to each other on her dining room table. From the drawer she took forks and knives and from the pantry, paper napkins.

Jake set the food down and looked at her. "I hope you like sausage and black olives."

"Except for anchovies, I never met a topping I didn't like." His lazy grin started chain reaction shivers inside her and she decided now would be a good time to sit.

"What are you drinking?"

She couldn't believe she'd forgotten to ask. "Just water."

He handled it, then took the other chair. While he'd filled glasses, she'd filled their plates with wedges of pizza and antipasto salad. They ate in silence for several moments.

She met his gaze. "Thanks, Jake."

"What for?"

"Dinner."

"You're welcome."

She set down her slice of pizza and wiped her

mouth. "I have a confession to make. Actually a couple."

"Uh-oh. That sounds bad."

"Not really. First of all, I was afraid I'd get home and find you and Emma gone."

Something flickered in his gaze. "The idea crossed my mind," he admitted.

"Why didn't you?"

"I'm not sure. What's your other confession?"

"I'm not proud of this, but I was sort of glad you had a bad day taking care of Emma. That you felt out of your element and ready to tear your hair out after dealing with a needy infant."

"Why?"

"So you'd throw in the towel—or the diaper as the case may be."

"Why?" he asked again. "So you could have things your own way?"

"It would make the situation easier," she admitted. "You have a strong, take-charge personality. I can understand Holly's apprehensions where you're concerned." When he opened his mouth to say something, she held up her hand. "I didn't mean that as a criticism, merely an observation. And she's still young, a teenager, certainly no match for you."

"I have nothing against Holly," he said. "But the welfare of this baby comes first, before her or Dan."

"I absolutely agree," she said.

"I hope that didn't hurt too much."

"What?"

"Agreeing with me about something." One corner of his mouth curved up.

"It only hurts when I laugh."

And that was her dilemma. It wasn't to have her

own way that she wanted him to throw in the towel. It was so she didn't have to see him and share joint custody. Because he was making it appallingly easy to slip into a false sense of security. She couldn't afford to get comfortable with him—be attracted to him or enjoy the give and take of their banter. If that happened, she had a feeling she could get hurt big time.

Two days later, Jake was standing in Rachel's kitchen humming while he waited for the drip coffeemaker to stop dripping so he could have a cup. He was happy as a clam at high tide to be leaving her place. Their agreement was to stay at the ranch on her four days off and he was anxious to get Emma home.

"Did I hear you humming?" Rachel stood in the doorway.

"Maybe. Why?" he asked, ignoring the punch-to-the-gut sensation he always seemed to get when he looked at her.

"A humming Jake Fletcher is a frightening thing. It could be a sign that three days of being cooped up with two women has taken a toll on you."

"Nothing I can't handle."

"So you're not one of those cowboys who needs lots of land under starry skies? What does the song say? 'Don't fence me in'?" She put her hands on her curvy hips and tilted her head to the side, studying him. "I figured the lack of space here must be getting to you by now."

"I didn't say it wasn't getting to me, just that I can handle it."

Tougher to handle was the sight of her in her sleeveless white cotton blouse tucked into denim shorts. Not a particularly tempting getup, but it sure did a number on his pulse rate. But he was ninety-nine percent certain it was nothing more than sharing these cramped quarters with her.

She smiled her sunshiney smile. "I'm glad we haven't driven you over the edge."

"Not a chance."

Although that all depended on which edge she meant. The edge of sanity? Or seduction? He was as sane as the next man. But thoughts of her in his bed weren't far from his mind after sharing her prissy, feminine space. Lace and candles everywhere along with dishes of dried flowers and stems that made the place smell like a hoity-toity gift shop. But it didn't manage to cover up the sweet smell of shampoo that clung to her blond hair or the scent of her skin after her evening bath.

Her pattern was to bathe just before going to bed. He'd seen her afterward, that first night, her cheeks flushed, hair wet and slicked away from her face, no make-up, short terrycloth robe that revealed as much as it hid, letting his imagination fill in the blanks.

She was big on bubbles; he'd seen all kinds displayed around the bathroom. If only he could get the image out of his mind—her wearing nothing but those bubbles, skin all pink from warm water and scrubbing. Because the apartment was so small, her scent was everywhere. The fragrance of her conjured images of her pretty face and trim little body. And the worst torment of all: what did she wear under that itty-bitty robe? He couldn't get those images out of his mind.

He'd tossed and turned on the itty-bitty futon, trying to sleep. Then Emma had awakened about 3:00 a.m. When he couldn't settle her, Rachel had come in to relieve him. But in an apartment the size of a closet, there was nowhere to get away from her and therefore, no relief in sight.

If she'd been cold and bitchy, it might have nipped his budding fascination. He could have gone on the defensive in a heartbeat. But she'd been polite and gracious. Sweet and funny. The first night he'd arranged pizza. The next evening she'd brought home take-out chicken. Last night they'd eaten chili she'd thrown in the crock pot before leaving for work. And it had tasted pretty darn good.

But he refused to get sucked in. Contrary to the popular saying, the way to this man's heart was not through his stomach. His heart wasn't up for grabs. Because he wouldn't trust any woman, especially one like her who made a habit of interfering. Was Jake itching to get back to the ranch? Damn right he was.

"So, are you all packed up and ready to go?" he asked.

She shook her head. "Emma's sleeping."

His muscles tensed. "How's that?"

"She took her bottle and fell asleep."

"You're pretty good at picking her up without waking her."

"That's not necessary. Since I didn't have a chance to get our things packed."

"Anything I can do to help?"

"Where's the fire? I've rushed out the door the last three mornings. It's a luxury to be able to take my time." She yawned and shook her head. "Besides, I'd rather not crash around getting stuff together and disturb Emma's nap."

His muscles tensed and his gut tightened. It felt like she was stalling. "Emma's a pretty sound sleeper."

"Maybe, but why take a chance." She met his gaze

and her eyes narrowed at what she saw. "Look, Jake, if you need to get back to the ranch, why don't you go on ahead? I'll meet you there when Emma wakes up, and I get my act together."

Her act? The concept felt like a negative to him and grated on his last nerve. Was Rachel up to something? "You wouldn't be trying to change our established ground rules?"

"And how would I be doing that?" she said, putting her hands on her hips.

"By not coming to the ranch."

And maybe skipping out of town. Easy, Jake, he cautioned. Dial it back a notch. She had a job and responsibilities. If she was going to split, she'd have done it before now. But he'd learned the hard way that women didn't always do what you expected. His own mother had done things behind his back. She'd interfered and connived. It had been as unexpected as it was hurtful. No woman would take him by surprise again.

"This is not a ploy to alter our agreement." She sighed. "If anything this is me enjoying the luxury of dragging my feet. And I want Emma to have a good nap. She'll be a much happier little girl. So, if you're in a hurry, go on ahead. Emma and I will meet you there—"

He shook his head. "I'll wait for you."

"Okay, then." She pointed to the baby's car seat sitting in the entryway. While she'd been putting in her time at work, she'd left it with him in case he needed to go out with Emma. "While we're waiting, maybe you could put her seat in my car."

"Or mine?" he said, watching her reaction.

"Or yours," she agreed. "But after that first day

you spent with her, I got the impression silence was a religious experience for you. I thought a little peace and quiet might be in order.''

He'd have thought so, too. Oddly enough, he liked having the little girl close by. It was Rachel he needed to distance himself from. "I'll put it in the back seat of my truck.''

"Okay,'' she said, turning away to go into the kitchen. "But don't say I didn't try to give you a break.''

That would be the day. Her femininity was driving him crazy. Probably because it was so effortless and elemental. He just hoped the ranch had enough space to take the edge off her effect on him.

He grabbed the car seat and took it to his truck parked in the area set aside for visitors. After taking out his cell phone, he dialed his foreman at the ranch.

"Hello?''

"Clint, it's Jake.''

"Hey, boss. What's up?''

"I'm coming back today.'' He glanced over his shoulder to make sure he was alone in the lot.

"Things are fine here. If you need more time away, boss—''

"No,'' he interrupted, glancing over his shoulder again to make sure Rachel hadn't followed him outside. "I'm bringing Rachel Manning and the baby with me today. But there's something I want you to do for me.''

"Name it.''

"While Rachel is at the ranch, I want you to make sure the hands keep an eye on her. She's not to leave the property without me. If she tries, I want to know about it.''

"Will do, Jake," Clint answered. "I'll get the word out to the boys."

"And make sure they know to keep it under their hats."

"Got it. See you later, boss."

"Okay."

Jake put his cell phone in his shirt pocket. He knew from his foreman's tone that the man had questions. But Jake wasn't about to answer them. He had enough of his own questions to choke a horse.

All of them about Rachel, the interfering buttinski who tied him up in knots.

Chapter Five

Rachel pulled her compact car in behind Jake's four-passenger truck. When she walked up beside him, he was lifting the baby's carrier from the back seat.

She peeked in on Emma. "She fell asleep."

"Yeah," he said.

When he met her gaze, there was a look in his eyes she couldn't read. Was he thinking she could have awakened the child and let her finish her nap in the car so he could have gotten back to work sooner? Maybe she should have, she thought, feeling a small prick of guilt. But it hadn't felt right to wake a peacefully sleeping baby so he could keep the two of them under surveillance.

Rachel met his gaze. "She just fell asleep because of the motion of the truck. It won't last long—the nap, not the truck. I'm beginning to see her patterns."

"I'm glad one of us is." He nodded toward the front porch. "Before she switches gears and wakes up, let's get you settled inside."

"Okay." She cocked her thumb toward her car. "I'll get our stuff."

"No. I'll show you around first, then come back and bring everything in the house."

He did have a tendency to take over, Rachel thought. But it was darn hard to fault him for it when he was being a gentleman. Babies needed a lot of stuff, and she was no slouch herself.

"I'm looking forward to the ten-cent tour," she said, glancing at the large, two-story house with buttercup-yellow siding and white trim.

"I think it's worth two bits at least."

From this vantage point, the porch, complete with railing, looked like it went all the way around. Following behind Jake, who carried Emma in her car seat, Rachel walked up the steps and inside. Into the lion's den, she thought, looking around. And it was one heck of a den. She looked up and noticed an oak railing across an open space upstairs.

Her sandals clicked against the wide tile entryway. On the left there was a living room with overstuffed green sofas facing each other across an oval coffee table. On the right was a dining area with an oak hutch and matching ball and claw-foot table with—she counted—ten chairs. Straight ahead was the biggest family room/kitchen combination she'd ever seen, with a river rock fireplace that took up an entire wall. A dinette rested in a nook and perpendicular to it was an island sink and bar with four stools.

It was just wrong for a bachelor to have a house this cozy yet put together. "How do you do it? Keep the place so *clean?*"

"I have a housekeeper who comes in once a week.

She does the grocery shopping and keeps the pantry well stocked.''

"Good to know." She was beginning to feel woefully inadequate. It was a load off her mind to know he had help.

"I'll show you the upstairs—and your room," Jake said.

A stairway was tucked in the corner of the family room and she followed him as it turned once, then opened onto a large game room with a pool table in the center.

"That way," he said, pointing to the left, "is the master bedroom."

"Your room?"

"Yeah." He turned and walked down a hall and past several rooms. At the end was a bathroom with bedrooms on either side—a Jack-and-Jill arrangement. "This is where you and Emma will stay. The rooms are large. You'll have lots of space."

Which he hadn't had at her apartment. Rachel tried with everything she had not to feel sorry for him. He'd been warned and had chosen to stay overnight at her place. A fact she'd been unable to ignore. When space was sparse, it was hard not to notice the large, attractive man filling it. If not for twelve hours at work to blunt the intensity of her notice, she wasn't sure what would have happened. She was profoundly grateful that his house had a lot of room to put between them.

Rachel poked her head into the first bedroom and saw a queen-size oak four poster bed with a floral comforter and coordinating bedskirt. A matching dresser and vanity sat at right angles to each other on the other walls. This must be hers. In the other room, she caught her breath at what she saw.

Surprised, she stared at Jake. "There's a crib in here." She glanced around. "And a matching changing table. And a matching armoire."

"Yeah."

"Everything matches." She looked into the baby bed. "Winnie-the-Pooh bumper pads, quilt, sheets and even a mobile." She pointed to the wallpaper border on the pale yellow walls. "All Pooh, all the time."

He moved his shoulders as if he was uncomfortable. "Nice to know you're up to snuff on your cartoon characters."

"When did you do all this?"

"You mean did I run right out after the court's decision?" One corner of his mouth quirked up.

"I guess that's what I meant."

"As soon as Dan told me Holly was pregnant, I fixed up this room for the nursery." He set the infant carrier beside the crib and a tender expression softened his features when he leaned down and tucked the receiving blanket more snugly around the sleeping baby.

"Why?" she asked.

He met her gaze. "I like Pooh."

"No. Why did you do it?"

"Because she's a Fletcher and I'm her uncle. I want her to have the best."

"Hmm," she said, noting the baby monitor on a shelf by the changing table. Peeking into the walk-in closet, she saw the generous space was crammed with baby paraphernalia—stroller, high chair, swing, diaper bag, disposable diapers in several different sizes, toys. His niece had the best, but only if she lived here on the ranch. Was it his way—subtle, or maybe not so subtle—of controlling the situation?

She looked at him. "What did you do? Call up the baby store and say deliver one of everything?"

"Kind of," he said with a shrug. He glanced at Emma. "Should we leave her there or put her in the crib?"

"By that you mean will *I* put her in the crib. And the answer is yes." She tipped her head to the side and studied him. "I have a feeling you've waited a long time to see her in there."

A sliver of guilt stabbed Rachel as she gently lifted the dozing baby and settled her on her back in the bed. She knew Holly thought Jake was controlling and believed he was trying to squeeze her out of the picture. Rachel wasn't so sure what, if anything, he was up to. But she was here because someone had to make sure that when Holly came back her baby would be waiting for her.

Rachel turned on the monitor and stuck the receiver in her pocket. "I don't think she'll sleep long. But if I've learned anything from Emma, it's that nine times out of ten, she'll make a liar out of me."

"Truer words were never spoken."

They left the door open and retraced their steps, going downstairs into the family room.

"This is a wonderful house, Jake."

"My parents built it when my mother was pregnant with Dan." He glanced around, a faraway look in his eyes. "I was a teenage accident and they got married. But after settling in, they tried for over ten years to have another baby. Finally, they figured it wasn't meant to be and decided to build the house instead. A month into construction she found out she was going to have a baby."

"Isn't that always the way," Rachel said.

He stuck his fingertips in the pockets of his jeans. "When Dan was a year old, my dad died in a freak ranching accident."

"I'm sorry." She put her hand on his arm, wishing with everything she had that his eyes weren't sad and his story wasn't a tearjerker. The look on his face was the one that got to her every time. Apparently she needed more practice in ignoring it. "So you were— what? Thirteen when he died?"

"Yeah." He moved away from her touch and rested his booted foot on the raised hearth, bracing his forearm on his thigh. It was as masculine a pose as she'd ever seen and her heart stuttered. Then she noticed a thoughtful, sort of wistful look on his face.

"Are you wondering if things might be different if your dad had lived?" she asked.

His gaze snapped to hers. "How did you know?"

"Because I think about things like that—about how my life would have been different if my parents had raised me instead of my grandmother."

"What happened to your parents?"

"They died in a small plane accident when I was six."

"I'm sorry."

She shrugged. "It was a long time ago. And mostly I don't think about what might have been. Mostly."

"If it matters, you turned out all right," he said.

"That's nice of you to say even though I know you don't believe it." She held up her hand when he opened his mouth to say more. "I'm not fishing for a compliment. I'm just trying to say that I know you're worried about Dan, but he'll be fine."

"Dan and I were always close. Mom died when he

was seven. I practically raised him. It feels like it's been just him and me for a long time.''

"So you have more of an emotional stake in how he turns out than most siblings.''

"And what happens to him. I only want him to be happy.''

"You said your parents were teenagers when you were born. Maybe the men in your family find their soul mates before turning twenty.''

An odd look stole into his eyes, something dark and intense. "I doubt that.''

"Is it possible you resent Holly? That you see her as interfering in your relationship with your brother? Changing the dynamics?''

He shook his head. "Don't go psychobabble on me. The last thing I'd do is interfere—'' He stopped and studied her. "Don't give me that look. Offering her a place to live is not interfering. And if she's the one for Danny, I'd be the first to welcome her to the family. Not like—''

"What?''

"Never mind.'' He met her gaze. "Actually, I was wondering about me. If things in my life would be different if my father had lived.''

"You turned out all right,'' she said, repeating his compliment about her.

"Did I?'' He rubbed a thumb along the oak mantel. "That's debatable. And not what I meant. He left Dan and me to be raised by our mother.''

She'd taken psychology classes in college and remembered that the same sex parent has the greater impact on a developing child. And to lose that parent at the tender age of thirteen, just when he was on the brink of manhood, must have been a devastating blow for Jake. There she went again, her heart bleeding for someone in need. Where was the on/off switch when she needed it?

But the dark look on his face made her terribly curious about what was going through his mind. And it wasn't just his expression. His behavior had her acutely puzzled.

Earlier, he'd been determined not to let her out of his sight while Emma was in her care. Otherwise he would have taken her suggestion to let her follow him to the ranch when Emma woke from her nap. Instead, while the baby slept, they'd had breakfast together and packed up what she thought she'd need for four days at his ranch. As pleasant as the meal and the companionship had been, she'd sensed his tension.

He didn't trust her as far as he could throw her. It could be his nature, but somehow she didn't think so. Something or someone had made him this way. Did he blame his father?

She looked up at him. "You make it sound like your father deliberately died and left you to be raised by wolves. I'm sure if the fates had given him a vote, he would still be here."

He met her gaze and a slow, sexy half smile curved up the corners of his mouth. "You think?"

"Yeah, I think." She smiled back.

He should do that more often, she thought. It was amazing how the smallest bit of humor erased the lines of tension around his eyes and mouth and lightened the dark look. Was it only humor? Or was it because he was on his turf and back in control?

Dirty and dusty, Jake walked through the back door, into the laundry room on his way to the kitchen. He opened the door and there was Rachel with her back to him. In cotton shorts and a tank top, she was standing in front of the open refrigerator. Well that was a sight he didn't normally see when he came in from work at the end of a long day.

The fact that he didn't trust her could almost make him ignore the pure male appreciation of her trim back, small waist and shapely hips. But the sight of her bare legs made him hot all over. And the fact that the sensation was getting stronger after three days and nights of her presence really ticked him off.

Turning, she smiled and said, "I thought I heard your truck. Hi, Jake, how was your day?"

"You know, Rachel, the court ordered us to live together. You don't have to pretend to be polite."

"'Hi, Jake, how was your day?' she repeated thoughtfully. Then she met his gaze. "Yeah, I can certainly see why a remark like that could turn you into Crotchety, Cranky and Crabby, three of the seven dwarfs from the dark side."

And didn't she have a knack for making him feel ridiculous. "I didn't mean—" He let out a long breath. "You don't have to act like—"

"A wife? Significant other?" She rested her hands on the hips he'd admired moments ago. "I'm not pretending. The fact is we're stuck with each other."

"Until the kids come back."

"Right. And I'm trying to make the best of the situation. So let's start over. Hi, Jake. I had a great day. I put Emma in the stroller and we had a long walk, got some fresh air. I showed her the barn and the horses and probably her first cow. She was so impressed, it wore her out. She took a nap for several hours allowing me to do laundry and cook dinner. And how was your day?''

"Long." Especially after a lousy night's sleep. Because he couldn't stop thinking about her being under the same roof. So much for his theory that more square footage would take the edge off his attraction.

"You must be starved. Dinner's ready. I've been keeping it warm.''

Of course she'd cooked, like last night and the night before. Earning her keep, she'd said. It was almost worth having her here for the experience of walking into the house and smelling dinner on the stove.

"What are we eating?'' he couldn't resist asking.

"Pot roast, mashed potatoes, green beans and home-made biscuits.''

His mouth watered and it wasn't just on account of the food. "Sounds good. Where's Emma?''

How had this woman completely skewed his focus? He was supposed to be protecting his brother's child, he reminded himself. Not distracted by a great pair of legs and a sweet smile.

"She's dozing." Rachel pointed to the baby swing in the center of the family room, gently moving back and forth. In the suspended seat, Emma was secured and safely propped up, although her head tilted slightly to the side and her eyes were closed. "That contraption is to a mother what the gamma knife is to a neurosurgeon.''

Mother? Is that how she saw herself? His gut tightened but he forced himself to relax. That battle was for another day.

He hung his hat on a hook in the laundry room, then closed the door behind him. "I'm not sure I quite get that but I'm guessing you like the swing.''

She nodded. "It gave me time to make dinner. While we waited for you, I was going to give Emma her bath. I think doing it in the evening soothes her at the same time it wears her out. She's practically sleeping through the night now."

He'd looked in on the two of them sleeping before he'd left the house that morning.

"I heard her about four," he said.

"Did she wake you? I'm sorry. I know you get up before God and I tried to get her settled before she disturbed you."

He shrugged. "It's a busy ranch. I need to use every hour in the day."

She folded her arms beneath her breasts, drawing his gaze to the bare flesh above the curved neckline of her T-shirt. He'd been starved when he'd walked in the kitchen. He was still hungry, but it had nothing to do with food.

"I'm going to clean up," he said.

She nodded. "I'll give Emma her bath."

Without waiting for her, Jake went upstairs and into his room. He closed the door and stripped off his clothes, then turned on the shower. He stepped in without waiting for the water to warm. A cold blast was just what his body needed. What the hell was wrong with him? Every damn time he was in the same room with Rachel, he felt like he'd spent way too long on a bucking horse—as if his brain had smacked once too often on the inside of his skull and had stopped functioning.

That wasn't completely true. He could still think, but his thoughts were filled with her. And he had his friend, Judge Olivia Edwards to thank for the fact that he was stuck with Rachel.

After letting the cool water pound on his head for a long time, he washed quickly then got out of the shower. He dried off and put on a clean shirt and jeans. Opening his bedroom door, he heard Rachel's soft voice, then her laughter drifting to him from Emma's room. The sound was like a magnet pulling him in. Instead of heading downstairs like he'd planned, he went down the hall.

Wearing nothing but a diaper, Emma was on the changing table, her arms and legs waving for all she was worth. Rachel stood beside her, smiling down. "You're such a pretty girl, yes, you are," she said, in that soft, singsong voice.

Tender feelings stirred inside him and he wasn't sure where the ones for Emma left off and the ones for Rachel began. He moved closer. Standing beside her, he realized the postbaby bath fragrances of lotion and powder didn't quite conceal the scent of Rachel that tied his gut into knots.

She looked up and grinned. "Jake, you have to see this. She's just started smiling."

"Yeah?"

"It takes a lot of work, but if she's in the right mood, she smiles. Watch."

She tucked her thumbs into Emma's tiny hands and automatically the little fingers curled around them. Smiling, she leaned in close. "Hey, pretty girl. You smell so good. Did you like your bath? Did you splash water all over the bathroom? Yes, you did."

She bent over and kissed the baby's tummy with a smacking sound. Emma reacted with a squeal.

"Did she just laugh?" he asked.

Rachel looked up at him with wide eyes. "I think so. Let's just try that again and see."

She bent over and repeated the actions with the same result. "I think that was almost definitely a laugh."

"I think you're right."

For the next several minutes, Rachel played with the baby. Sounds spilled out of her like happiness that was too big to keep inside. It was impossible to keep from smiling. As he did, he absently touched the tiny one piece sleeper Emma would wear to bed. An unfamiliar sensation of contentment settled over him. It was nice having the baby here. And Rachel.

Suddenly he realized how lonely he'd been. And not just since Dan had been gone with Holly.

His brother was growing up—and away. From the time he'd earned his driver's license, he'd spent less and less time at the ranch. Jake had expected and understood the need of a teenage boy to be out with his friends, studying, socializing. But now—seeing this woman and child—he realized how empty his life had become.

When Rachel trailed a finger down Emma's tummy, the baby shifted to the side as if it tickled. Her toothless grin didn't waver as she made gurgling sounds.

"Does that feel good?" Rachel cooed. "Do you like that?"

God help him if she touched him like that. Jake knew he would be putty in her hands.

Rachel looked up, almost as if she'd heard that thought. "I don't know, Jake. I've been reading baby books on age appropriate behavior and I think she's a little early on the whole smiling and laughing thing."

"Really?"

He stared at her in the light from the baby lamp beside her. She was all slender angles and soft curves.

Small nose, kissable lips. Then she looked up at him and he felt the full force of her appeal. His gut caught fire—spontaneous combustion. All he could think about was touching his mouth to hers, just to see if she tasted as good as he imagined.

"Really," Rachel said. "I think she's exceptionally smart. Maybe even gifted."

"Tomorrow she'll be walking and next week skipping grades in school," he said.

"Go ahead and mock me. But there's something in her eyes, which are going to stay blue, by the way. She's got an intelligent look that hints at her astronomical IQ."

"Of course. What else would you expect from a Fletcher?"

She blinked up at him, then looked away frowning. Damn. This time he hadn't meant to, but he'd effectively reminded her that his claim to the baby was the strongest. It hadn't been his intention to shut her out. God help him, he'd been enjoying the comfortable companionship. And he kicked himself for chasing the light from her eyes.

"Yes, she's definitely a Fletcher," Rachel said, grabbing the sleeper. She put one of the arms on Emma, then lifted her and dragged the garment underneath her little body.

Maybe it was for the best, Jake thought, tamping down his feelings of attraction and frustration. Rachel was casting some kind of spell over him. Just as well he'd nipped it in the bud. The other day when she'd first arrived on the ranch, he *had* been wondering if his life would be different if his dad had lived. But not for the reason she thought. His dad would never have let his mother take away his child.

Rachel was funny, fun and wonderful with Emma. She seemed too good to be true. And she probably was. He couldn't trust his senses or his judgment. For God's sake, his own mother had deceived him. He'd never dreamed his own flesh and blood could do what she'd done.

It was just a matter of time until Rachel tripped up. The trick was not letting her innocent act lower his defenses. He would never give a woman the opportunity to betray him again.

Chapter Six

After her twelve-hour shift at the hospital, Rachel arrived home tired and happy to be there. She'd missed Emma. And, as much as it annoyed her, she acknowledged the ribbon of anticipation curling through her at the prospect of seeing Jake.

She walked through her apartment door. "Hello?"

Looking around, she didn't see him, but she was pretty sure he was here. The evidence of controlled chaos was everywhere. Sleepers, clothes, diapers, bottles—oh my.

"Jake?"

"In here."

If he'd said "in here" at his house, she'd have had trouble narrowing down his whereabouts. But in her space, there weren't too many places he could be—either the spare bedroom or the bathroom. She walked down the hall and checked the latter first. Bingo. There he was, dark hair mussed, as if he'd run his fingers through it countless times. In his trademark jeans and white cotton shirt with the long sleeves rolled to just below his elbows, he looked way better than she would have liked.

She took a deep breath, willing her voice to be normal and neutral. "Hi. Where's Emma?"

He lifted his chin toward the other room. "Crib."

"So what are you doing?" she asked, watching him put the baby's tiny tub on the countertop. Beside it rested washcloth, shampoo and baby body wash. She met his gaze. "Don't tell me you're going to be a brave little soldier and give Emma a bath?"

"Nope. I was getting everything ready for the second team." One of his dark eyebrows rose. "That would be you."

"Ah." She nodded. "Bathing her really isn't hard, you know. I could show—"

"I'll take your word for it."

"Who'd have guessed a big strong guy like you is afraid of a tiny baby?"

"Not afraid of *her*," he countered. "Just her, water and soap all at one time."

"Come on, Jake. I'll bet you've ridden horses with a nastier disposition than Emma. Or faced down mountain lions poised to rip your throat out."

He leaned a hip against the cabinet. "Aren't you being a tad melodramatic?"

"Me?" she said, touching a hand to her chest. "Heaven forbid. Maybe exaggerating a little."

And for a very good reason. She'd finally teased him out of the snit he'd been in since moving "Operation Baby-sit" back to her place. Or maybe it had started right after their last night on the ranch when they'd stood side by side and watched Emma giggle and laugh. Until he'd effectively reminded her that she had no familial connection to the little girl. But she got that the remark was meant to distance her. And he'd continued to put up walls between them afterward. The extra effort was probably because he didn't know whether to relax and go with the flow. Or treat her like Public Enemy number one.

But since she'd done two of her three shifts, day after tomorrow they were pulling up stakes to go back to his ranch. She figured this sign of a thaw in his disposition was partly due to their pending change in venue and only two more nights on the futon that barely fit his frame. She couldn't blame him for being grumpy, even though he'd agreed to this.

And she hated the quirk in her personality that allowed her to see both sides of an issue. She wanted to be completely hostile to the man Holly believed was trying to take away her baby. But Rachel had a feeling there was more to Jake than a need to be in control, bedroom blue eyes and a bod to die for.

"I have never faced down a mountain lion. Although I've seen my fair share of snakes," he added.

"Any of them go for your throat?" she asked.

One corner of his mouth lifted. "Probably wanted to. Fortunately for me they're vertically challenged."

"Snakes can't jump?"

"Nope. Although they can drop from trees, rocks and other high places. But we digress."

"Yes, we do," she said. Something that happened to her often since meeting Jake Fletcher. Keeping her mind on task was tough after taking one look at him. "Although changing the subject works in your favor since you were defending your honor. Trying to put a positive spin on taking the coward's way out."

"I'm not a coward. Bathing is on a need to give

basis. You were due home so there was no need for me to give it.''

"Actually, I'm glad you waited. I love giving her a bath. She enjoys it so much. It's easy to get a smile out of her.''

A shadow drifted into his eyes. Was he remembering the last time they bathed her at the ranch?

"While you do that,'' he said, "I'll see about dinner.''

"Does that mean you're cooking or dialing the phone?''

"Depends on whether or not you want something edible.''

"I'm starving,'' she said, her gaze settling on his mouth.

Her pulse skipped as she realized she would very much like to know how it felt to kiss Jake Fletcher. She knew he didn't trust her, although she didn't understand why. But that didn't alter the fact that she wanted to experience the feel of his lips against her own, and she wouldn't say no to a moment folded in his strong arms.

"I'll make a phone call,'' he said, his voice husky.

There was something in his eyes, an intensity that made her wonder if he'd known what she was thinking. But that was nuts. Because, technically, she didn't know what she was thinking or why she was thinking it. All she knew was that ever since she and Jake had begun their court-ordered joining at the hip, she'd felt a yearning open up deep inside her. A sense of things in her life falling into place. And the conviction was growing stronger every day.

"Okay. I'll bathe Emma.''

He nodded and walked away. Rachel breathed a

sigh of relief then peeked in on the baby who was on her back in the crib. The little girl was wide-eyed, intently watching the revolving mobile Jake had switched on for her. Rachel ducked into her bedroom and changed out of her work clothes and into yellow knit shorts and a matching tank top.

She undressed the infant and carried her across the hall to the bathroom. After taking a quick inventory to make sure everything was there, she filled the tub with warm water and immersed the baby who started to gurgle and coo.

"Do you like that?" she said, smiling. She braced the little girl's head and neck on her forearm and gripped the tiny upper arm. "Does that feel good? Your uncle Jake is really cute, but he's a big chicken. This is easy, isn't it, Emma?"

Sounds from the living room indicated Jake had answered the door. She heard his deep voice and knew he was talking to someone, probably whoever had delivered dinner. It was nice to know food would be on the table when she finished. After that, a bottle before putting Emma down for the night. Then she and Jake…

What? Could talk like an old married couple with a baby? She remembered his reaction on the ranch when she'd innocently asked about his day. Was she just being polite? Or did she have a subconscious need to make more of this than she should? Heaven forbid.

"Emma, I think I've finally flipped out," she whispered to the baby who gave her a heart-tugging, adorable, toothless grin.

They'd only been in this arrangement for a short time and already Rachel was feeling the effects. She was attracted to Jake, no question about that. But why?

Because her usual type had a sob story and sad eyes and so did he? That was partly true. From time to time a sadness crept into his gaze, but the rest of the time he was controlling and dictatorial. That should be enough to cancel out her attraction. But it wasn't.

The only other explanation was that her bargain with the devil had opened up the wound she'd thought had healed a long time ago: her craving for a traditional family—father, mother and little girl.

When she watched Jake cradle Emma in his strong arms, the phrase "daddy's little girl" would creep into her mind. What would it have been like to experience that? She couldn't remember. Not that she'd spent much time with her father. He was career military and had to go where he was sent. Then her parents had died before she'd had time to make memories to tuck away. She was grateful for her grandmother who'd taken her in, and Rachel loved the older woman very much. She felt like an ungrateful wretch when this yearning crept over her. But she couldn't help the feelings.

The situation with Jake was as close to a traditional family experience as she could remember. She'd always yearned for traditional. That must be why she was so acutely attracted to him.

"Dinner's served," he said, poking his head into the bathroom. "Whenever you're finished with the full body immersion."

"Mission nearly accomplished." Rachel glanced over her shoulder and looked at him.

She was almost used to the skip of her heart at the sight of his dark hair, blue eyes, square jaw and nice mouth. It was highly unlikely she would ever know how it felt to kiss Jake Fletcher. Because underneath this uneasy truce of theirs, he still thought she was interfering in something that didn't concern her.

But Dan and Holly needed her help. She was giving them a chance because she shared their concern that Jake wouldn't. And everyone deserved a second chance. They would use theirs to take over the care of their baby, then the three of them would become a family. A little bubble of envy tinged with sadness expanded inside Rachel.

Obviously it would take a little longer to learn to live with that feeling and get it under control.

The next night Rachel arrived home an hour early. The hospital's patient census was down and she'd completed her work, so her supervisor had okayed her early departure. She stopped in front of her apartment door and breathed deeply.

Taking a moment, she tried to think of a way to tell Jake that Dan and Holly were okay without breaking her promise to keep their whereabouts secret. They'd called her today from a pay phone, and it wasn't the first time. They called her cell number while she was at work, deliberately avoiding Jake. Every time she spoke to them, she asked them to at least let her tell Jake they were safe. And each time they begged her not to, afraid he would somehow make her tell him where they were.

Everything was fine, and they needed a few more weeks. She'd felt there was no choice but to agree. Against her better judgment. Because she had no wish to hurt Jake and felt strongly that he had a right to know about his brother. But she'd promised the teens, and she wouldn't betray that trust.

When she let herself into the apartment, she heard the low, masculine voice from the other room.

"Jake?" she called automatically. When there was no answer, she figured he hadn't heard. She dropped her purse and keys on the coffee table and hurried down the hall. He was in the bathroom—bathing the baby.

"Jake?"

He glanced over his shoulder, his jaw rigid and eyes narrowed. Sweat beaded on his forehead. "I'm giving her a bath," he said.

Rachel moved in close enough to see around him and check on Emma. She didn't look happy. Waving her arms up and down, she splashed water in her eyes, startling herself into crying out.

"It's okay, little girl," he said. Then he shot Rachel an angry look. "I thought you said this relaxes her."

"It does—if the person doing the bathing isn't tight as a primed slingshot. She feels your tension and gets more tense. Children mirror what's going on around them. It's called autoexacerbating syndrome."

"I don't give a rat's behind what it's called," he said tightly.

"Sorry. Try to relax."

Easier said than done, she thought, noting the stiffness in his broad shoulders and the corded tension in his neck as he resolutely held the squirming infant.

"Do you want me to—"

"No," he snapped.

He took the washcloth resting on the side of the tub and washed Emma's face, then dragged it over her head. When her wiggling caused her to slip, he swore softly and caught her in both hands. Then he settled his palm on her back, his fingertips supporting her head. Her little legs pumped in agitation and Jake wore a look of grim determination.

Rachel wished he would let her do something. Why wouldn't he?

After what seemed an eternity, he said through gritted teeth, "I'm done."

He lifted the baby out of the water and cradled the wet, whimpering infant against the front of him, soaking any part of the shirt that hadn't been soaked before. Without a word, Rachel handed him the towel and he awkwardly wrapped it around the baby. He carried her across the hall and set her down on the changing table.

"It's okay, Em," he said, voice tense. "You probably won't believe this, but that hurt me a lot more than it did you."

Boy, wasn't that the truth, she thought. The baby was fine, but he was a wreck. Without a word, she handed him skin cream, then a diaper and a one-piece sleeper to dress the little girl.

He held Emma still with one hand and undid the buttons on his shirt with the other. After shrugging out of it, he tossed the wet material on the futon then picked up Emma and nestled her against his shoulder. Rachel knew Jake needed to comfort more than the baby needed comforting.

"I've got a bottle ready," he said and carried her into the living room. He sat on the couch and positioned her in the crook of his elbow, then picked up the bottle and put the nipple in her mouth. Eagerly she latched on and started to suck.

When Jake finished feeding Emma, he took her into the other room and put her down for the night.

"You want to tell me what that was all about?" Rachel asked when he returned to the living room.

He stopped buttoning the fresh shirt he'd put on. It hung open revealing the muscular expanse of his chest covered with a dusting of dark hair. Rachel hated that she wanted to touch him and see if it was as coarse and crisp as it looked.

"What are you talking about?"

"I thought you knew I was teasing about the whole bath thing. I wasn't issuing a challenge."

"It was to me. I don't like not being able to do everything for her," he said. "I could almost see you wanting to snatch her away when the bath was finished."

"Yeah," she agreed. "It was hard to hold back. If you'd waited, I could have—"

"What?" he asked, a dangerous gleam stealing into his eyes. "Taken over? Done it better? Faster? Saved Emma from a traumatic experience?"

"If you'd let me finish," she said through gritted teeth. "Emma's fine. It's you I was worried about. And I wasn't talking about taking over. I could have helped, talked you through it, given you pointers. But you shut me down. Why is it so hard to ask for help? What are you trying to prove? Why do you have to be in complete control?"

"Because then no one can cut me out of the picture," he snapped, eyes blazing.

"I've never tried to do that," she said. But even as she said it, she wondered if he was talking about *this* picture. "I know you don't trust me, but I've never done a thing to warrant that opinion. What happened to make you so suspicious?"

He shoved a hand through his hair. "I had a child, Rachel, a son. When I was seventeen."

"Oh, Jake—" Whatever she'd expected, it hadn't been that. Abruptly, Rachel sat in the wing chair that, fortunately, was right behind her. "Where is he?"

"He was adopted."

"Look, Jake. I know from your behavior there's more to this story. And I can't help thinking you're starting in the middle."

He nodded. "I already told you my dad died when I was thirteen. Afterward, I turned to my mom. So I told her my girlfriend was pregnant and I was going to marry her. I needed her permission. Mom said she would handle it. But the next thing I knew Janine wouldn't take my calls. I tried to see her, but her folks would only say she went away to school and they wouldn't tell me where. Mom tried to convince me the situation was being handled, and I should be grateful to be out of it. She told me to forget the whole thing and move on."

"I don't know what to say." Rachel was stunned. "Obviously, you couldn't forget it."

"Could you?" He ran his fingers through his hair. "About a year after my son was born—it was a long time before I even knew his actual birthday—"

"What's the date?" she asked quietly.

"July 16." There was anguish in his gaze. "Anyway I ran into Janine in Sweet Spring. I confronted her about what happened and asked why she'd refused to take my phone calls. She was shocked. Her folks hadn't told her I'd tried to contact her. And she'd left messages for me with my Mom."

"You never got them," she said, stating the obvious. What kind of parents conspired against their children like that?

He shook his head. "Janine said she thought I'd turned my back on her and our son. She felt abandoned and her parents convinced her the best thing was to give the baby up for adoption."

"I thought biological fathers had to sign away their rights for that to happen."

"My rights were signed away, but it wasn't by me."

"But how?"

"My mother. She forged my signature on the papers because she knew I wouldn't sign away my rights to my own flesh and blood."

"Oh, Jake—"

"Wait, it gets better." He rested his hands on his lean hips. "I was eighteen by now and figured I had some legal status as a man. I convinced a legal aid attorney that my rights had been violated and he agreed to represent me in a suit to get my son back."

"What happened?" The question was purely rhetorical.

"The court ruled in favor of the adoptive couple. They'd had him for almost a year. He'd never known any other parents. The judge said it was his responsibility to do what was best for the minor involved. And it was clearly best that my son remain in a stable, loving home with two mature parents as opposed to me—a single teenager. Even though the ranch was successful, without my mother's support the court decided he'd be better off in his current situation."

"You must have been devastated."

He looked away for a moment and the muscle in his cheek contracted. "I barely spoke to my mother again after that. And she died six months later. She said it was for the best and someday I'd thank her. She was wrong. I'll never forgive her for what she did to me.''

"Have you looked for your son?"

He nodded. "I know where he is."

"Does he know you? Have you spoken to him?"

"No. Because he's happy, healthy, athletic and getting good grades in school. If he wants to meet me, I'll be there. But I realized it would only hurt him to butt into his life. As long as he's going along okay, there's no good reason to do that.''

"I can't begin to imagine what you've gone through." She shook her head and let out a long breath. "But I have to ask you one question."

"What's that?"

"The court system completely trampled your paternal rights. I practically begged you to keep this a private matter. Why in the world did you take legal steps to get custody of Emma?"

"Figured lightning couldn't strike the same place twice." He lifted one shoulder. "I'm a man now and it wouldn't be so easy to walk all over me. And I had a friend sitting on the bench. Should have been a slam dunk.''

"Yeah." She looked up at him. "I really wish you hadn't told me what happened to you."

"It wasn't my idea. You demanded answers."

And she'd gotten them; his story was a doozy. She knew now why he didn't trust her and she couldn't find it in her heart to blame him. His own mother had betrayed him in such an elemental way.

Unfortunately, without trust, it was impossible for love to grow. The woman had probably thought she was doing what was best for Jake. Unfortunately, she'd robbed him of a child, she'd stolen any chance he might have had for a happy, fulfilled life. Rachel's heart ached for him. All she could do was try to show him she would never betray him.

"Yes. I demanded answers. And now I'm sorry you told me." She stood up and walked over to him. "Because I really want to dislike you. It would be so much easier if I could just write you off for being a control freak. Now I have to acknowledge that you've got good reasons for your inappropriate behavior."

"What behavior would that be?"

"Trying to get Holly to move to the ranch. Leaning on the kids to do things your way. Insisting Emma belonged with you. Spouting all that stuff about family. Not letting me out of your sight while I'm taking care of Emma."

"Rachel, I—"

She put her hand on his arm, a gesture meant to soothe, but the warmth of his skin, the corded muscles moving beneath her palm excited her instead. "Now I know you're a nice guy whose actions are a reflection of what happened to you in the past."

She met his gaze and sighed. Here we go again, she thought. He had a five hanky sob story if she'd ever heard one. And she knew she was going to regret this but she couldn't help it.

Rachel put her arms around him.

Chapter Seven

Jake tensed at her touch. Since the morning when he'd come to Rachel looking for his brother and found a woman who looked like a walking sunbeam, he'd thought about her like this—snuggled up nice and close. But never because she pitied him. He curved his fingers around her upper arms and started to push her away.

When he made the mistake of looking into her eyes—brown eyes that sympathy darkened to chocolate—he tried to tap into the white hot anger he'd felt when she'd first interfered in his life. He couldn't find it; he'd gotten to know her. There was a sweetness about her. Some innate quality of gentleness that made it damn hard to generate irritation, let alone distance and distrust.

When she slipped her hand past his parted shirt and pressed her small, warm palm against his bare chest, he knew this battle was lost. He wasn't particularly proud of the fact that something as superficial as lust had splintered his self-control. But it couldn't be helped. He could no more turn away from her now than he could lasso a tornado.

He tunneled his fingers into her hair and when she innocently slid her tongue over her upper lip, he was a goner. ''Aw, hell—''

Cupping her face in his hands, he lowered his mouth to hers. He tasted surprise on her lips and doubt. Or maybe that was the way her fingers curled into her palms at his waist. And apprehension—he felt that when she shivered because no way could she be cold.

The heat was instant and consuming as he slid one arm around her and drew her slender curves full up against him. At this moment he didn't care that she could probably feel how much he wanted her. As he deepened the kiss, her breasts nuzzled his chest and the pleasure of it nearly dropped him to his knees.

He wanted more.

Tracing the seam of her lips with his tongue, he urged her to open to him. When she did, he wasted no time entering her, tasting the moist, honeyed sweetness of her mouth. Her soft moan was like tossing kerosene on embers. Then she surprised him with shy, gentle touches of her own.

She trailed her tongue along the roof of his mouth. A low, rough sound he hardly recognized as his own rumbled in his throat. Then he felt ripples of awareness course through her. She'd accepted him and that turned him on in a major way. His breathing went from idling to hard and fast in the blink of an eye. He was awash in nerves and feelings, swamped by the overload from his senses. Good God, what was she doing to him?

Rachel savored the feel of his lips against her own.

She found security in his strong arms followed by a heady awareness when she felt his erection pressed against her. Proof that he wanted her. He trailed nibbling kisses over her cheeks and jaw then lavished attention on a spot just beneath her ear. Heat enveloped her everywhere his mouth touched. It was like a fire and consumed all her oxygen. She couldn't seem to draw enough air into her lungs and her breathing grew more rapid.

Tension coiled low in her belly as her body readied to be one with him. She pressed herself to his bare chest and all she could think was how much she wished her blouse was gone, that there was no material between them. She wanted his flesh pressed against her own. The wanton thought brought her up short. She'd never felt so out of control. The realization worked better than a cold shower.

She broke the contact of their mouths and couldn't stifle her satisfaction when he groaned. There was nothing she wanted more than to go on kissing him. She ached for him to lift her into his strong arms and carry her into the bedroom. To take his sweet time undressing her. To tangle her sheets with the sweet love they could make.

But it was a fantasy that could never be. Deliberately, because she didn't want to let him go, and carefully, because she knew she had to, she removed her arms from around his neck. She took a step back, then another.

"Rachel?" His voice was little more than a hoarse moan.

She touched her fingers to her kiss-swollen lips. When she realized her hand was shaking, she shoved it into her pocket. "Jake, this is—"

"Don't say wrong," he ordered.

Even though it is, she wanted to say. "Okay. I won't say it."

"Good."

She forced herself to meet his gaze and the doubt she saw there. "You have to admit that was weird."

"I don't have to admit anything."

"You're going to make me be the grown-up, aren't you?"

"I'm not exactly sure what you mean by that." He ran his fingers through his hair.

The movement brought her attention to his still unbuttoned shirt. If he was any kind of gentleman, he would button it the heck up and hide the broad expanse of pure temptation. With an effort, she swallowed her desire. "One of us has to be mature about this."

He put his hands on his hips and speared her with a look. "I thought we were doing a fine job being mature. Tell me you didn't like what we were doing."

She took a deep breath. "I wish I could."

"So you did like it?" he pressed.

"It was far and away the best kiss I've ever had. Are you happy now?"

"Yes." A slow, sexy smile of satisfaction curved his lips. He reached for her.

Her heart lurched, telling her she was still in a lot of trouble here. She took another step back. "I will even go so far as to say I'd like nothing better than to do it again."

"I can arrange that," he said, one long stride canceling out her backward progress.

"Jake, you've got to help me here. I won't deny I'm attracted to you."

"I sort of figured that out on my own."

"But that doesn't mean we have to act on it."

"Unless you can come up with a pretty good reason *not* to act on it, I—"

"Please don't go there." She shook her head. "Look, Jake, you've got to help me out here and back off. Promise you won't do it again."

"And just why would I want to do that?"

"Because if you kiss me, I'm pretty sure it won't stop there. You must know that taking such a step would further complicate an already difficult situation."

He stared at her for several moments, then let out a long breath. "I wish I could say you're wrong about that."

"Good. Then we're on the same page. I'm sorry things got out of hand."

"I'm not." He folded his arms over his chest as a dark intensity claimed his features. "And I won't apologize. If you're expecting it, you can wait for a Texas snowfall in July. I'll never regret that kiss."

"Okay. Good."

But was it? Rachel had the strangest feeling she'd just cut off her nose to spite her face. But it was necessary for self-protection. He'd just revealed a betrayal of profound personal proportions. Her heart hurt for him. But giving in to her attraction would be a monumental mistake. He would never trust a woman. Without trust, it was impossible for love to grow.

Rachel realized she needed to build sturdier walls around her heart to keep Jake out as long as they were forced into constant contact while taking care of the baby. Her life would go back to normal in a few weeks. It would be best if she didn't fall hard for a Fletcher. And that included Emma *and* Jake.

"Tell me again why you went to all the trouble of having my friend Ashley watch the baby so you could take me out to dinner." She glanced around, then looked at the fish entree arranged so artfully on her plate. "And such an elegant place, too."

Jake was wondering the same thing. It had been two weeks since he'd kissed her and she'd asked him to promise not to do it again. Yet their table was tucked into a shadowed corner of the restaurant that he would have to call romantic. Rachel sat at a right angle to him, her forearm resting on the fancy white tablecloth only inches from his. She was wearing a black cotton halter dress, modest but seductive at the same time. Which made no sense. Somehow it suited her to a *T*.

Just looking at her made his gut knot with frustration of the sexual kind. But that wasn't an answer to her question. And staring at her beside him, all big eyes and soft hair looking as if a man had run his fingers through it while loving her, wasn't helping.

Why had it been so important to arrange this evening out?

She met his gaze and light from the candle in the center of the table flickered over the curve of her cheek. Romantic music played in the background. He could have picked a place that specialized in Texas barbecue and country western tunes. Or even a hometown buffet. But he'd chosen an upscale French restaurant, the kind that impressed women because the food looked great and that men hated because the portions were fit for midgets. It would leave him hungry in more ways than one.

He set his fork down beside the beef entree on his plate. There was plenty of white space and not a whole lot of beef. She'd ordered some fish thing he couldn't identify.

And she was still waiting for him to respond to the question. Jake could give her the safe answer—it had been over a month since they'd negotiated their arrangement to take care of the baby and they both needed a change of scene. The real reason was a lot more complicated. He took a roll from the basket, then settled the cloth napkin around the others to keep them warm.

"Like I said, you needed a night out." Better safe than sorry. He spread butter on the inside of his bread and watched it melt. Sometimes when he looked at Rachel his insides did the same thing. "You've gone back and forth from your apartment to the ranch. You've done nothing but put in time at the hospital, then take care of Emma." And me, he added silently, thinking about the laundry that she did, and the dinners on the table when he walked in after a long day. "The truth is, Rachel, you coochy-cooed the baby once too often and I was starting to worry."

She laughed. "It's not really that bad. And I love taking care of Emma."

What about me, he almost asked, but managed to stop himself just in time. "It shows."

"I'm going to miss it," she met his gaze and there were shadows in her eyes. "When the kids come back, I mean."

"I wish I knew where Dan is."

"And Holly," she reminded him.

"Yeah," he allowed. She was Emma's mother and he cared what happened to her. He had to remember it took two to make this situation. "I'd like to know my brother is okay. I've got a thing or two to say to him about not calling."

"I'm sure they're fine." Rachel held the stem of her wineglass and turned it without meeting his gaze.

"I'd just like to know."

She hesitated a moment, then said, "If they weren't, you would have heard. No news is good news. Bad news travels fast." Her voice sounded strange, not quite her bright, optimistic tone.

"What do you know about the speed of bad news?"

"More than I'd like." She took a sip of wine. "My parents were killed when I was just a little girl."

"I'm sorry," he said automatically.

"It's not a current tragedy." She lifted one shoulder. "My father was career military—an Air Force pilot. He was stationed overseas for a year and I'd just started first grade in a different school from where I went to kindergarten. My mother didn't want me disrupted again, so we stayed behind. But mom missed him so much she left me with my grandmother and went to him."

There was a sad, wistful tone in her voice and he couldn't stop himself from reaching over to cover her small hand with his own. "What happened?"

"They were in a small, twin-engine plane that went down in bad weather."

"That's rough." Under his fingers, her hand jerked, then stiffened, but she didn't pull away—something she'd been doing ever since he'd kissed her.

"My grandmother told me I shouldn't be sad. They loved each other so much and they were together." There was anger and deep hurt in her gaze. "But I was alone."

"I'm sure that's not what they wanted, Rachel."

"My head agrees with you. But my heart— I wish she'd loved him less and me more." She pulled her hand away. "If she hadn't had to be with him, she would have been around for me." She met his gaze. "That sounds selfish and whiney. It's the shallow truth and I'm sorry."

"Don't be. It's honest. Just keep in mind accidents happen. Your mother expected to come back to you *with* your father." He looked at her. "'What ifs' and 'if onlys' will make you crazy, Rachel. Trust me, I know."

She looked at him for several moments, then her mouth curved up. "Has anyone ever told you you're way too rational?"

"Yeah. I can be annoying that way."

She laughed, then the amusement faded. "You can joke, but I'm serious when I say I don't ever want to care as much as she did or be in a position where I have to choose."

"I understand you feel strongly about being left behind. But that makes me curious about why you're so determined to help Holly. She left her baby."

"Because I didn't have my mother, I know how important it is for Emma to preserve her bond with Holly. Trust me, I'm aware the situations are different." She let out a long breath. "Fortunately, I have my grandmother. She's been good to me and I love her very much. But Holly has no family to turn to."

He decided this wasn't the time to point out that he had tried to be there. But to be honest, he had to admit his offer was for Dan, not Holly. "Yeah, family is what it's all about."

"I couldn't agree more. But Gram is of a different

generation. She's old-fashioned and doesn't always understand times have changed. I've missed having my mother to talk to.''

"What about your father?'' he asked. He thought that slip said a lot about her.

"I hardly remember him; he was gone a lot. But my mother was always there for me, until she died. I was pretty little, but the trauma of hearing that news is always with me. There were things I needed her for and she wasn't around.''

"Like what?'' he asked.

"You don't want to hear that.''

"Yeah, I do.''

Oddly enough, Jake sincerely meant that. He'd bared his soul about the baby that was taken from him. He hadn't meant to, but anger, adrenaline and something about Rachel had made him open up. Somehow sharing his past had made his soul a little lighter. Suddenly he wanted to know more about what made her tick.

"Okay.'' She sighed. "Remember in court when the judge asked me why I'd befriended Holly and was taking care of her baby?''

"You said you're a bleeding heart liberal who's hard-wired that way.''

She nodded. "And, trust me on this, being a bleeding heart liberal isn't all fun and games. I've had some bad experiences along the way.''

"Tell me about them.''

"You want me to humiliate myself for no good reason?''

"What if I promise to track down the bad guys and beat them up for you?''

"How can a girl refuse an offer like that? Okay.''

She thought for a second. "I remember once stopping at a gas station and a guy asked me for money." She slid him a wry look. "Before you go off on me, he was nicely dressed in a suit and tie and said he'd forgotten his wallet. He needed to fill up his tank to get to work. He had a wife and a brand new baby and he would send me the money if I gave him my address."

"And did you?"

"Of course." She sighed. "I went into the convenience store and when I came out the car was still there with someone else filling it up and the guy in the suit had disappeared with my money."

"That could have happened to anyone."

"Maybe. But it didn't always happen with strangers. I've had relationships."

He didn't want to hear this. The idea of her with another man tightened his gut and ticked him off. And convinced him he wasn't annoyingly rational. He was a damn lunatic.

"Two out of three times, it cost me something. A stereo, my favorite videos, money."

He wondered if she'd ever lost her heart. "I guess you picked the wrong guys."

"Thank you for stating the obvious. One guy cost me a birthday. In high school government class Rob Turner asked to look at my term paper—just so he could see the format. He xeroxed it, then accused me of copying from him—word for word."

"So why do you keep reaching out?"

"Because I can't stop myself." She shrugged. "I can't turn my back on someone who needs help. Besides, I don't always get burned."

"Two out of three is too many. You need a keeper. Someone to protect you from the Rob Turners of the world.'' Jake frowned. ''So what happened? You said it cost you a birthday.''

She nodded. ''My grandmother grounded me. I missed my sweet sixteen birthday party. And while that in itself would be enough of a trauma to a girl, it's quadrupled in my case. Technically, I only have a birthday once every four years.''

''You want to run that by me again.''

''My friends Jordan and Ashley and I were born on February 29.''

''Interesting.''

''You have no idea. This year we celebrated in New Orleans and had the weirdest experience. We met a Gypsy after we managed to retrieve a brass lamp that some hoodlum had shoplifted from her.''

''Not too bright to go toe to toe with a hoodlum.''

She grinned. ''Literally. Jordan tripped him.''

Concern for her safety churned inside him, even though it was after the fact. ''What happened to the hoodlum?''

''He got away. But that's not the interesting part. The Gypsy said we should rub the lamp and make a wish.''

''Isn't it usually three wishes?''

One corner of her mouth lifted. ''There were three of us. We each got one. Do the math.''

''Right,'' he said with a grin. ''What was yours?'' he prompted.

''It was— A baby,'' she said, meeting his gaze. ''The whole situation was bizarre and the words just popped out of my mouth.''

''That's weird.'' Subconscious weird, he figured, since Holly had been living with her at the time. A coincidence. ''So you want children?''

She nodded. "But, I believe in a family with a father *and* a mother. A girl especially needs her mother to warn her about guys like Rob Turner."

"Why? You said yourself you're hard-wired this way. If experience hasn't taught you caution, what makes you think anything your mother said would have made a difference?"

Shadows slid into her eyes. "That's just it. I never got the chance to know."

This explained a lot, he thought. Why she was going to the mat to protect Holly's rights to Emma. Why she wanted so badly to believe Holly would come back. But his experience proved that mothers didn't always do the right thing. And a man would be better able to warn a daughter about what guys were capable of.

But all he said was, "Kids need a father, too."

"I don't dispute that," she said. "Nature is set up that way. Otherwise babies would be created by spontaneous combustion instead of— Well, you know."

Yeah, he definitely knew. He'd thought about "you know" a lot since that kiss. The hardest thing he'd ever done was keeping his promise to back off. And he hadn't lied when he said he would never regret it.

"Jake, I know we disagree about this. But Dan and Holly are trying to see if they can handle the responsibility of themselves alone, without a child. They're trying to do what's best."

"What's best is for them to get married. I told him so."

"I thought we put that issue to rest when you first brought it up." Her eyes grew wide. "Did you mention it again to Dan before he took off with Holly?"

"Yeah." He sipped his water. "It's the right thing to do."

"Your mother thought she knew what was best, too," Rachel pointed out. "And she took matters into her own hands. Don't do that to Dan."

"I'm not," he snapped. "If he marries Holly, they can live on the ranch. I'll help him, and he can still go to college. He'll have to give up his athletic scholarship, but he won't lose his child."

"You love him very much and you're trying to give him everything."

"What's wrong with that?"

"Nothing. But as soon as he made the choice to have sex he was making grown-up decisions. Now he's in a situation. Right or wrong—whether you agree with him or not—the choices and decisions are his. Don't do to him what your mother did to you. Don't shut him down under the guise of giving him everything."

Anger coiled in his gut. She had no idea what she was talking about.

"This isn't the same thing at all." He put down his fork and glared at her. "It's completely different with Dan and me."

"Is it?" She wiped her mouth with the cloth napkin and set it beside her plate.

"Damn right it is."

"Okay."

"Don't patronize me, Rachel."

"I'm not doing that. I'm trying to get you to respect Dan and Holly's choices. There's no point in arguing that this is in any way a good situation. But those kids are working hard. For some reason they felt the need to get away from you."

"I would take care of them both."

"That's Dan's job. He's struggling to be a man,

Jake. You should know better than anyone that having choices taken away from you is not the way to do that."

"I'm not like my mother."

"I don't believe you'd go behind their backs, but in your own way you're trying to get them to do what you want them to. You think you know best. It's in your genes. And you're pushing for a do-over through Dan."

"You couldn't be more wrong."

"If you say so." She nodded. "But that doesn't change the fact that the choices are theirs. Emma is their baby. She's not yours—or mine."

There was conviction in her words, right up until the last part. Then, as if she'd really heard what she'd said, her expression turned profoundly sad. Jake believed everything she'd said was baloney and her know-it-all attitude grated on his last nerve. In spite of all that, the look on her face, as if she'd lost her best friend, made him want to tug her into his arms. So what the hell was that about?

He stared at her and realized three things. One, she was way off base about him acting like his mother. Two, Rachel cared for the baby more than she would probably admit.

Three, and this was the weirdest of all, he was going to have to work harder at feeling nothing for Rachel Manning.

Chapter Eight

Jake hadn't said two words to her on the way back to the ranch, and he'd disappeared without going into the house. Rachel smoothed over his absence, then walked her friend to her car. "Thanks for watching Emma. You said she was a little fussy?"

"Yeah, a little. Then she fell asleep. I think she missed you." Ashley tucked a strand of curly red hair behind her ear. She hesitated, then said, "Has it occurred to you that she's your wish come true?"

"It crossed my mind," Rachel admitted. "But not only is that too weird, she's only mine temporarily. So the answer is—no. I think this whole situation is nothing more than coincidence."

"Must be," her friend agreed a little too quickly. "Did you and Jake have a good time tonight?"

"That depends on your definition of good time. For a carefree dinner out, the answer is no. If you're talking good-time-group-therapy session it was a rousing success."

Rachel winced at the memory of telling Jake about her mother leaving her behind. As if it was still a recent tragedy. Remembering her vehement responses, she hoped he didn't think she was an emotional cripple. Then she'd proceeded to tell him he had deficient genes on his mother's side. She was lucky he hadn't walked out and left her to hitchhike home. Home? She didn't mean that. She meant generic home or back to the ranch. No way was she feeling at home in his place.

"Don't worry." Ashley opened the door of her compact car. "I'm not going to ask what a good-time-group-therapy session is. Just let me remind you what happens when you take the emotionally wounded under your wing."

Rachel winced again. She'd told him about that, too. Holding up her hand, she said, "Not necessary. Tonight I took a walk down memory lane—and hit every speed bump along the way. I warned Jake about my track record."

Ashley put her hand on the top of the open door. "Actually, I wasn't thinking about Jake. He's a big boy. He can take care of himself. It's you I'm worried about. How can you not keep from falling in love with that precious little girl?"

Rachel had been worrying about that, too. "This time I'm not going to get hurt. That's all there is to it. I knew it was temporary going in. There won't be any surprises. I constantly remind myself that I'm nothing more than a place holder—until her mother gets back. My motto is no emotional involvement."

"Since when have you ever listened to yourself," Ashley said. "This is *you* we're talking about, Rach. The woman who wants to mother the world."

She really didn't want to go where this conversation was headed. She'd managed to keep it from her friends that Jake had kissed her. But after tonight's conversation she felt raw. It would be too easy to blurt out that she'd liked kissing him way too much.

Rachel folded her arms over her chest. "What's this I hear about bad boy Max Caine running Caine Chocolate?"

"What have you heard?" Ashley asked warily.

"I do work in the hospital. I know Bentley Caine walked out against medical advice and his grandson showed up looking for him. It's no secret that Caine Chocolate Company employs a good number of Sweet Spring citizens. So it's all over town that the very same grandson you had a crush on before he left ten years ago is now back running the company for his grandfather."

"Temporarily," Ashley clarified. "And don't think I didn't notice that neat sidestep you did to change the subject. Now it's my turn. I don't want to talk about it any more than you want to talk about Emma and her uncle breaking your heart."

"That works for me."

"It's getting late, I really have to go." Ashley leaned over and hugged her friend. "Ouch," she said, fishing something out of her breast pocket. She handed over the baby monitor. "I think this belongs to you. Don't leave home without it."

"Or at least the house." Rachel laughed. "Thanks again for watching her."

"Anytime." She slid into the car and shut the door.

Rachel watched Ashley head down the road. Even after the car disappeared in a cloud of dust, she was reluctant to go inside. Normally during the month of

July, Texas nights didn't cool off, they just got dark. But there was a coolness in the air making the evening pleasant. The now familiar scent of hay and horses drifted to her and she didn't wrinkle her nose and mentally go *"eww."*

She figured she must be getting used to the wide open spaces. One of the best parts was the full moon that bathed everything in a bright silver glow. Without nuisance light, the stars glittered in the sky. The beauty of Jake's ranch and the contentment she felt when she was here filled her with a deep sense of longing.

She heard Emma's snuffling sounds, then deep breathing indicating that she was sleeping. Glancing at the contraption in her hand she decided this baby monitor was state of the art, thanks to Emma's spare-no-expense Uncle Jake. Where was he anyway? She remembered their "light" dinner conversation and his rational comments.

Who said cowboys were simple, Rachel thought. He was one extremely complicated man. And she was beginning to feel guilty about some of the things she'd said to him. Maybe she had some fence mending to do. She glanced around. In the distance, by the corral, she saw movement, a flash of white. She realized it was Jake's shirt.

"Here goes nothing," she mumbled, sticking the monitor into the pocket of her sundress.

As she walked, heading up the rise to the barn and corral, dirt slid into her sandals, reminding her she was out of her comfort zone in more ways than one. But she had to do this.

"Hi. What are you doing out here?" she asked after stopping beside him and resting her arms on the top of the split rail fence. She felt the movement of his shoulders in a shrug and figured maybe she'd stopped close enough to get burned.

"It's a nice night. I like the outdoors." His tone was cool, neutral, hard to read. "I saw Ashley leave."

"Yeah. She has to work in the morning."

"Don't we all." He removed his booted foot from the bottom slat of the fence, as if he was going to walk away.

"Wait, Jake," she said, putting her hand on his forearm. She felt the corded muscles tense and pulled away. "I didn't get a chance to thank you for dinner."

"Don't mention it."

"I have to. Arranging dinner, including someone to watch Emma— I think you're very sweet and thoughtful."

"Yeah, I'm one hell of a nice guy. When I'm not disrespecting my brother's choices or thinking I know what's best for everyone." He looked down at her and nudged his hat up with a knuckle.

"I guess I had that coming." She sighed. "I'm sorry. I should have kept my opinions to myself. One thing about us bleeding heart liberals. We walk a fine line between doing good and butting in. I believe I crossed that line tonight and not in a good way."

"You think?"

"I had no right to say those things to you. There are women who would scratch my eyes out for saying they've become their mother after all."

"No kidding. And people who live in glass houses shouldn't throw stones."

"What does that mean?" she asked, her irritation piqued. After all, she was trying to apologize.

"You've obviously got unresolved abandonment issues with your own mother."

She turned toward him and put her hands on her hips. "And you've been watching too many talk shows on afternoon TV." The ridiculousness of this conversation hit her and she grinned. "We're certainly a pair, aren't we? You've had too much mothering. And I haven't had enough."

"How does it feel to be the one on the psychiatrist's couch?"

"You tell me." Her smile faded. "I could be wrong, but in spite of the circumstances under which we've been thrown together, I felt we'd developed a friendship."

"You're not wrong."

"Then I don't get it. I said I'm sorry and you're obviously still ticked off at me."

"I'm not mad at you. I'm mad at me."

"Why?" The admission took her totally by surprise.

"Because you said I'm acting like my mother and I still want to do this."

Before she realized what he planned to do, he'd reached out and pulled her against him. He folded her into his arms.

"You promised not to kiss me again," she said, surprised at the thread of desire in her voice. His mouth was scarcely an inch from her own. The tempo of his breathing had increased—just like her own.

"Technically, I didn't promise anything. I agreed that kissing you again would complicate an already difficult situation."

"So why are you doing this?"

"Because there's something going on between us. If you deny it, you'd be lying through your teeth." In the moonlight, his gaze burned into hers, daring her to do it. "I can't ignore it anymore."

She knew exactly what he meant. And she couldn't ignore how right it felt to have his arms around her. All her warnings went up in smoke, seared by the smoldering expression in his eyes. And how very much she wanted to kiss him back. "Okay. You win. Let's complicate the heck out of this situation."

One corner of his mouth lifted. "Put your arms around my neck."

She stood on tiptoe and did as he asked. His hold on her tightened as he pressed her to the hard length of his body. Then his lips touched hers and she couldn't suppress the small moan of pleasure in her throat. It was like coming into port after an eternity of aimless drifting on a large, lonely sea. If she'd never known the exquisite pleasure of his kiss, she might have been able to resist. But she did know and decided resistance was a colossal waste of energy.

He threaded his fingers into her hair and cupped the back of her head as he made the contact of their mouths firmer. She heard his raspy breathing and felt the rapid rise and fall of his chest. The evidence of his desire connected with a motherlode of yearning deep inside her. Heat arced between them, threatening to make her go up in flames.

He pulled his mouth from hers and stared into her eyes, his breathing hard and heavy. Intensity crackled in his gaze. "What are you doing to me?"

"Nothing," she said.

"That's where you're wrong," his voice was hoarse and a thread of anger ran through it. "You've got me under some kind of spell."

"Wait a second, buster. Right back at you. I'll see your spell and raise you an incantation or two."

He grinned. "That's what I like about you, Rachel. You give as good as you get."

She blinked up at him. "Did you just admit you like me?"

"I already admitted we're friends, but it was probably part of that whole spell thing you've got going on."

"I see." She slid her hands from his neck, down over the muscular contours of his chest. "Far be it from me to wear out my welcome. I'll just take my spell and go home—"

"The hell you will," he said, tightening his hold.

A sound came from the monitor in her pocket. A little cough and a sneeze. Instantly, Rachel pulled it out.

"Ohmigosh. Emma."

"We better go in." Jake loosened his hold and stepped back from her.

"Yeah."

Rachel's feminine needs sat up and screamed "No." But checking Emma was her first priority. Although she did regret losing the warmth and security of Jake's arms. They started toward the house and he took her hand. The simple gesture was achingly sweet at the same time it tripped all her warning signals.

Once inside, he followed her upstairs to the nursery. Emma was awake and fussing so Rachel picked her up. She held the small, warm body snugly to her chest and the baby quieted. The feeling was amazing—to be so important to someone that just your touch and presence reassured them.

She looked at Jake and saw the dark expression in

his eyes. If she'd really and truly cast a spell, shouldn't it include a direct line to his thoughts? She wished she knew what he was thinking; no way would she ask. But the look on his face was a sobering reminder that this baby was his niece and Rachel was another woman interfering in his life. Not only that, she was lying to him. Chances were good he would never forgive that.

In spite of what she'd told Ashley, she loved this baby—more every day. It would be hard to turn Emma over to someone else when the time came. But Rachel loved the baby enough to give her back to her mother and father—because that was best for Emma.

Rachel sighed, wishing she could have stayed in the moonlight just a little longer. Under the stars, she'd been able to forget everything but the feel of Jake's mouth against her own. But she was in his house now where the harsh light of reality intruded.

There were battles ahead still to be fought. She could feel it.

Jake rested his forearms on the crib rail as he looked down at Emma, flat on her back in her crib. After quieting her, Rachel had excused herself for her own nightly bathing ritual. She'd taken the baby monitor with her because she'd told him it was her watch and he should go to bed because he got up before God, and God rolled out of the sack pretty doggone early. But thinking about Rachel in her bath would keep him awake even if he did go to bed.

He heard the sounds of water splashing. Since the bathroom was right next door, it was hard not to. Parts of his body were hard, too. How could he not be, thinking about her soft flesh covered in bubbles?

Would it be easier if he hadn't kissed her a little while ago? He shook his head. If he hadn't, he would still be thinking about doing it. Hell, he'd done it and all he could think about was how much he wanted to do it again.

Emma waved a chubby fist and when it brushed against her mouth, she latched on and sucked with a loud smacking sound. He grinned. Was every baby so beautiful? His chest felt tight suddenly, emotion squeezing his heart. She was his brother's child, for that reason alone Jake cared. But every day his love for this little girl grew and deepened. And no one knew better than he did that these were days Dan would never get back. Where the hell was he and why hadn't he called?

But somehow Jake couldn't regret that he'd had this time with Emma. And Rachel? Did lust count? Hell, he knew for sure he wanted her. But he didn't know how he felt about her.

"Is she all right?"

Jake stiffened at the sound of Rachel's voice behind him. He felt as if he'd been caught with his pants down, thinking about her the way he was. And those thoughts had kept him from knowing she was there. It kept him from noticing the sweet, floral scent that always surrounded her after her bath. He braced himself for the sight of her.

"She's fine," he said, turning to meet her gaze.

Standing in the doorway, she wore a short summer robe belted at the waist. Her hair was straight and damp and tucked behind her ears. Not a speck of makeup covered her face. But she was so damned beautiful she took his breath away. A blast of need slammed into him, so powerful that he curled his fingers around the crib railing. He should have known there was no way to brace himself for looking at Rachel.

"I wondered why you weren't in bed yet," she said.

There was no good reason to tell her the truth. It would give her way too much power.

He shrugged. "I heard her and came in to look."

"I wonder why she's not sleeping. Usually she's out like a light by now. Ashley said she thought Emma missed me. I wonder if us going out and leaving her with a stranger has thrown her off schedule. I've done a lot of reading. There are theories that babies as young as Emma notice differences in their surroundings."

Did that mean Emma was getting used to him and Rachel? As if the baby could read his mind, she let out a wail. Jake reached into the crib and lifted her into his arms.

"What is it, Emma?" At the sound of his voice, she let out another cry. "Okay. I get it. You want to go vertical."

He lifted her to his shoulder and supported her head with his hand. She rubbed her face back and forth against his shirt, restless. After a series of halfhearted cries, she wailed loudly.

Jake met Rachel's gaze. "Any ideas?"

"She could be hungry. I'll go warm a bottle."

He nodded and she turned away, leaving him alone with the baby. When Emma balked in spite of the upright position, he paced back and forth. It helped a little, but when he stopped, she revved up again, louder this time.

"Where's that bottle, Rachel?" he mumbled.

This wasn't the first time he'd been in this situation,

dealing with a fussy baby. But he was feeling more and more that there were times Emma preferred Rachel. During her twelve-hour shift he hung in there as best he could. But when Rachel got home from work, he'd let her take over. Just now, he'd sensed her tension when Emma cried, as if her maternal side was revved up and raring to go. He knew she wanted to take the little girl and comfort her, but she'd left the baby in his arms.

Emma wailed again. "It's okay, little girl. Reinforcements are coming."

Just then Rachel appeared in the doorway. She walked in and handed him the bottle. "Here you go."

"Thanks."

He settled himself in the glider in the corner of the room with Emma in the bend of his elbow. He put the nipple in her mouth. She latched on to it and sucked for a few moments, then opened her mouth and let loose with a high-pitched, frustrated wail. Jake looked at Rachel. "Got any other ideas?"

"Try again?" she suggested.

He did and the same thing happened. "You want to try?"

"Okay." She didn't hesitate, as if she'd been itching to get her hands on the little girl.

He stood and she walked over to him, her arms held out. As he slid the baby into them, he felt the softness of Rachel's breast through her robe. An arc of electricity shot to his groin and he figured he was going straight to hell. Or maybe he was already there. But the fact that he could be aroused by this woman under these circumstances made him a jerk or crazy. He wasn't sure which.

"Here you go, Emma." Rachel sat in the glider and

crossed one shapely bare leg over the other. She settled the baby and put the nipple in her mouth. With a deep, shuddering sigh, the little girl latched on and started to suck for all she was worth.

What had Rachel done differently? Absolutely nothing. Yet the baby was obviously content and not because of him. An odd sensation tightened in his gut and if he had to name it, he'd call it jealousy. How stupid was that? He couldn't be with her twenty-four hours a day. But neither could Rachel. It was almost fifty/fifty.

Even as he thought it, he knew it was a lie. At her place, Rachel always took the night feedings. She'd said the apartment was small and once Emma was awake, she couldn't sleep anyway. He hadn't protested, partly because Emma seemed more content with her. Partly because he'd caught a few more Z's that way. Was it his fault?

"I think she likes you best," he blurted.

Rachel looked up, surprise written all over her face. "Don't be silly."

"I don't think I am. Why else would she take the bottle from you and not me?"

"I don't know." She shrugged. "Maybe because she's overtired and unreasonable?"

"No."

"There are times when I can't quiet her, either."

He wanted to believe that. "How do you know what to do?"

She shook her head. "I just go through the checklist in my head—clean diaper, full tummy, possible gas discomfort. If I can't identify one of the above as a problem, I figure she needs to go to sleep. Babies aren't a big mystery."

Not if you knew the baby in question. She obviously did. He hated to admit that he was the blood relative, but Rachel was better at caring for his niece. Like she'd said, she mothered the world. He found watching her at it damned fascinating.

She met his gaze. "What was on your mind before? When I first came in, before Emma started fussing."

He wanted to pretend he didn't know what she meant. But he remembered. Some of his thoughts were about her naked in the tub. But when she'd walked in the nursery, Dan had been on his mind. "I was thinking about my brother. And what he's missing."

Rachel looked down at the child cuddled in her arms. "I know."

"It doesn't have to be this way. If only I knew where he was, I could convince him to come home and let me help."

"He's trying to stand on his own two feet. That characteristic reflects in a positive way on how he was raised."

"What about his running away? What about the fact he hasn't called? What does that say about his upbringing?"

"I think Dan knew you would make sure Emma is okay. Has that occurred to you? There's a bond between you two. Now he's asking for the gift of time. When they come back, they'll have the confidence in themselves to take their baby and make a family."

Her voice held a trace of sadness. He was a little surprised he recognized it. Maybe he did because he felt it himself. When Dan and Holly came back, everything would change. He was certain his brother would give up his athletic scholarship and marry Holly. Jake would convince her to make a home here on the ranch where she and his brother would raise the next generation of Fletchers. But that meant Rachel would be gone. The thought turned him inside out.

The worst part was that his feelings had nothing to do with lust. If only he could pin the blame there. But lust was a function of biology. Relationships were much more complicated. He'd worked damned hard at avoiding emotional entanglements. It took trust, and his mother had shown him all about that. But Rachel was breaking down his barriers on that score. And even with family around him, he would be alone. Again.

She was beginning to make him wonder if things could be different.

Chapter Nine

"Answer the phone, Jake," Rachel mumbled, holding the receiver to her ear. "Pick up, pick up, pick up."

When his cell phone voice-mail message came on, she waited for the beep then said, "Jake, it's Rachel. Emma's running a fever. I had a feeling something wasn't right when we had trouble getting her settled down last night. I've given her something to bring her temperature down and called the pediatrician. Because she's so little, Dr. Stern wants to see her so I'm going to run her into Sweet Spring. Meet me there if you can. If not, I'll call back and let you know what the doctor says. But Jake—I really need you."

She clicked the kitchen phone's off button. He hadn't answered, which meant one of two things—either he was too busy to pick up or he was out of cell phone range.

Her attention shifted to the fussy baby sitting in her infant carrier on the floor in the family room. Emma's normally bright blue eyes were dull and her cheeks flushed. Her pathetic cry said she didn't feel good; her expression said do something. This was the first time Emma had been sick and Rachel couldn't help being apprehensive.

Her heart caught as it hit her like a ton of bricks how big her feelings were for this little girl. In spite of her protests to Ashley—that she'd known it was temporary, she was just a place holder, her motto was no emotional involvement—here she was head over heels in love with this baby.

And where the heck was Jake? He might have trouble asking for help, but she didn't. More than anything, she wished he was here right now for moral support. The only thing worse than going through this infant health crisis was going through it alone.

"I guess it's just you and me, Em. But I promise you'll be fine. I'll take care of you. It's just that I would feel so much better if your Uncle Jake was here." She walked over and picked up the carrier. "Let's go, pumpkin."

She went out the front door and down the steps to where her car was parked. There was a chirp when she hit the keyless entry button, then she opened the rear door and dropped the diaper bag on the floor. After securing Emma's carrier with the seat belt, she saw the tears glistening on the baby's dark eyelashes and leaned forward to kiss her forehead.

"You're going to feel better in a little while, sweetie. Don't you worry. After we see the doctor, everything's going to be fine as frog's hair. And what the heck does that mean anyway?"

She shut the baby inside, then walked around to the driver's door and got in. Taking a deep breath, she put the key in the ignition, started the car and adjusted the air conditioner to keep Emma as comfortable as possible. There was a knock on her window, startling her. She expected to see Jake, but it was his foreman, Clint Davis standing there.

She put the window down. "Clint, hi."

"Miss Manning," he said, politely touching the brim of the brown hat covering his short, dark hair. He looked to be somewhere in his mid to late twenties. There were crinkles at the corners of his hazel eyes, a clue that he smiled often. His face was round, cheeks and nose permanently ruddy from working outdoors.

"Have you seen Jake?"

"Yes, ma'am. Early this morning. He said he was riding out to inspect the fences."

"So he is out of cell phone range."

Clint nodded. "Wouldn't be surprised. Anything I can do for you?"

"Tell Jake I have to take Emma into Sweet Spring—"

"Sorry, ma'am, I can't."

She blinked. That was weird. If there was one thing she'd learned about this ranch it was that all the men who worked for Jake Fletcher were loyal and unfailingly polite. It was completely out of character for this man to blow her off like that. Maybe he'd misunderstood.

"I know Jake's not here now. But when he comes back, if you see him before I do, tell him Emma is running a fever and I'm taking her to the doctor in town."

"That's just it, ma'am," he said, looking uncomfortable. "I can't let you go."

"Excuse me?"

"I can't let you take the boss's niece off the ranch."

A big, bad feeling dug in. "What are you talking about?"

"I have orders, Miss Manning."

"What orders?"

"If you tried to leave we were to stop you. And Jake was to be notified immediately."

Fury at Jake battled with her fear for Emma and Rachel tamped both down with effort. "Look, Clint, didn't we establish that Jake is somewhere and can't be reached?"

"Yes, ma'am."

"I left a message on Jake's cell phone that Emma is sick. I'm sure he wouldn't have a problem with me taking her to the doctor." But she had a problem with him and he was going to get an earful when she saw him.

"That may be, ma'am. But until I hear from the boss, I can't let you take little Emma there off the ranch."

Rachel couldn't believe this was the first time the issue had come up. They'd been sharing custody for over a month. But then she thought about it. His housekeeper brought groceries once a week when she cleaned. Rachel worked in town three days a week. If there was anything they needed, she made sure she brought it with her when she started her four day stretch on the ranch. She'd been content there with the baby, taking walks for fresh air, getting to know Jake better. The few times they'd ventured off the property, he'd always been with them. She'd never once tried to leave on her own. Her new best friends, solitude and peace, had kept her right where he wanted her.

"Look, Clint, do you understand Emma is sick? The

doctor is expecting us. That means, I have to leave the ranch.''

''I'm sorry, Miss Manning. I truly am. But I have my orders.''

Rachel put the car in gear. ''Then you can take your orders and stick them in your ear. I won't be kept a prisoner when this baby needs medical attention and Jake can't be reached because he's off playing with his cows.''

''Now, ma'am—''

Rachel didn't hear any more because she pressed her foot down on the gas and took off. Glancing in the rearview mirror, she saw the foreman staring after her. So, he'd been behaving in character after all. He was both polite and loyal—to Jake. A rush of anger fueled by betrayal, humiliation and injustice pumped through her. How dare Jake do this to her? How could he?

She'd taken great pains to play by the rules they'd set up. They'd agreed that friendship had grown between them in spite of the fact that he believed she was interfering. For goodness sake, he'd kissed her. Twice. And she knew he'd been as aroused by the experience as she. If he didn't trust her how—

That was just it. He didn't trust her. Silly her for thinking, even for a moment, that they could be friends. Or that his kisses had been generated by deeper feelings.

She was in a state of mad-as-heck and grateful to be there. Because when the adrenaline rush wore off, she knew it would hurt like hell.

Anxiety clawed through Jake. As soon as he'd heard Rachel's message on his cell phone, he'd hurried into

Sweet Spring. *Jake, I need you.* The alarm in her voice had been unmistakable. And the words tapped into a placc deep inside him where it felt good to be needed.

He parked his truck in one of the diagonal spaces in front of the pediatrician's office then got out and went inside the building. When he saw Rachel in the waiting room, he was both relieved and worried. She and the baby were the only ones there. Emma was sleeping in her carrier beside Rachel.

"I got your message when I was on my way back to the house for lunch." He took off his hat and sat down in a chair with the baby between them. "How is she?"

"Sleeping." Rachel put a hand on the carrier handle as if she expected him to grab it up and head for the hills. "We're still waiting to see the doctor."

"How come she hasn't seen you yet?"

"She fit us in. We have to wait our turn."

He glanced at the baby then at Rachel and realized she was answering his questions with as few words as possible and hadn't once looked at him since he'd walked in. A muscle jerked in her cheek and she had a death grip on the infant carrier. She didn't look like a woman who would have said *Jake I need you.*

Something was bugging her that had nothing to do with Emma being sick.

Just then the door separating the waiting room from the back office opened. "Emma Fletcher?"

Rachel stood. "That's us."

"Right this way."

Jake put his hand on the carrier to help her with it and she gave him a look so filled with hostility he felt as if he'd been slugged in the gut. What the heck had put a twist in her panties?

The nurse led them to an exam room and instructed Rachel to undress the baby. She took Emma's temperature and wrote the results in the chart. A few moments later, the door opened and the doctor walked in. Jake recognized Dr. Stern, a short-haired brunette with warm brown eyes. They'd brought Emma in once before for a well-baby check and the doc knew the circumstances of their situation.

"Our girl's not feeling well?" she said, looking at the chart.

"She's running a fever," Rachel said. "And she sounds congested, too."

"Let's take a look."

While Emma squirmed and whimpered, the doctor listened with the stethoscope she'd first warmed between her hands. She looked in Emma's ears then checked her throat. She asked if her diapers were wet; dry ones were a sign of dehydration. Rachel answered that they were and Emma was eating normally.

"You can dress her now." Dr. Stern draped the stethoscope around her neck and looked at them. "I think she has a plain, old-fashioned summer cold."

Rachel moved beside the exam table and diapered Emma, then slipped on her two-piece pink knit shorts outfit. "Doesn't she need some medicine? A prescription?"

"We don't want to overuse antibiotics. Otherwise when she really needs them they won't work."

Jake wasn't satisfied with that. "But, Doc, we're talking one time. Can't you give her something to get her back on her feet right away—"

"I could, but it wouldn't help. This is a virus. I know it's hard. When a child doesn't feel well we want to fix it immediately. But we need to give her immune system a chance to mature. We want Emma's body to learn to make antibodies. If we give her help, in the long run she won't be as strong. I can recommend pediatric decongestants to make her more comfortable.''

Rachel picked Emma up. ''I know what you're saying, Doctor. But—''

''It's amazing how fast babies can steal your heart,'' Dr. Stern said.

''What?'' Jake ran his fingers through his hair.

''You two are acting no differently from other parents.'' The woman looked at them and smiled. ''I'm on call for the county, and I see abandoned babies all the time. It's refreshing to see a situation where teens have family support and the space to make a rational and reasonable decision for a child and themselves.''

''You don't think what they're doing is irresponsible?'' Jake asked.

''Of course I do.'' The doctor slipped her hands into the pockets of her white lab coat. ''But at least they're trying to make a good decision in a bad situation. They didn't throw her away. Literally. Whatever happens, when they grow up and look back they can say they did their best. It's because of you two that they can really think about what they're going to do.''

''That's what Rachel's been telling me.'' And maybe there was some substance to her theory. Jake looked at her, but she wouldn't meet his gaze.

''I may be way off base for saying this—'' The doctor hesitated as she studied Rachel cuddling the infant. ''Try not to get too emotionally attached to Emma. Teens, especially girls, can be so unpredictable. They change their minds at the drop of a hat. It can be a difficult situation for everyone concerned.''

"She may change her mind," Jake said, "but she can't change the fact that Emma is my niece, my family."

"I'm aware of that," Dr. Stern said. "But the fact remains that you're not this baby's father and Rachel isn't her mother. And that could be a hard place to be."

Jake hauled the infant carrier from Rachel's car to the apartment. Her suggestion to stay in town, close to the doctor made sense to him. Her cold shoulder didn't. The night before they'd nearly gone up in flames under the stars. Now she was treating him as if he'd stomped the insides out of her favorite stuffed animal. He didn't know what was going on, but he intended to find out.

After she unlocked the front door, he went inside and set the carrier down on the floor. Emma was alert and in good spirits and he figured it meant her fever was under control. Rachel picked her up and took her into the other room. He followed and watched Rachel change Emma's diaper. Then she warmed a bottle and the little girl took it easily. After she finished, Rachel carried Emma into the other room and put her down for a nap.

When Rachel came out, he was waiting. He held out a canned soft drink. She hesitated and he thought she would refuse, but finally she took it, careful to avoid touching him.

"Enough of the silent treatment, Rachel. What's wrong?" He pointed a finger at her. "And don't tell me nothing. I've seen ice cubes with a warmer attitude."

"Did you talk to Clint Davis before you came into town?"

"No. As soon as I got your message, I hightailed it to the doc's. Why?"

She took a sip of her soft drink, then set it on the coffee table. "Because he told me about the standing order you left."

"There are a couple of standing orders—like no smoking in the barn."

"This is the one where I'm not allowed to leave the ranch without you."

Oh, boy. He'd completely forgotten about that. He'd also forgotten how cold her brown eyes could be when she was angry. He hadn't seen her this way since he'd first insisted Holly marry Dan.

Rachel put her hands on her hips and glared at him. "I can't believe you don't have anything to say."

"Like what?"

"A denial. An explanation." She shrugged. "Something?"

He let out a long breath. "You don't look like you're in the mood to believe anything I say."

"Try me."

"I left the order. But it was a while ago."

"Why would you do something like that?"

"It was when we first started taking care of Emma together. The first time we were going to the ranch. That morning, here in your apartment, I got the feeling you were trying to come up with an excuse not to live up to your end of the bargain. I was concerned that you might—" He ran his fingers through his hair. "Hell, I don't know. I guess I gave the order to hedge my bets. Just in case you decided to take off."

"Take off? Yeah, I can see where you might draw

that conclusion based on my personal history. Clint tried to stop me from taking Emma to the doctor.''

''He was only following orders.''

''How could you ask him to do something like that in the first place?''

''I hardly knew you then, Rachel. I couldn't believe you didn't have an ulterior motive for getting involved with Holly and Dan and the baby. What was I supposed to do?''

''Give me the benefit of the doubt?''

Jake met her gaze. ''It's hard for me to do that.''

''Okay. I guess I can understand that. But why didn't you rescind the order? When you got to know me? Or maybe you still think I'd do something selfish to cut you out of Emma's life.''

''I forgot about it.''

''Yeah. Right.''

''It's true.''

Yet he had no way to prove it, to convince her otherwise. He'd only been trying to do what he thought was right, to protect what was his. But from the first moment Rachel had set foot in his house—technically from the first moment he'd set foot in her apartment—she had destroyed his concentration. For God's sake, he had a ranch to run, business to conduct. And all he could think about was her sunny smile, her curvy little body, the way she mothered Emma, the way she fit so perfectly into his world. And then he'd made the mistake of kissing her. How the hell was he supposed to remember what he'd done before that?

She sighed. ''You know, it really doesn't matter whether or not I believe you. But this proves to me that Holly was right to be wary of you.''

''What's that supposed to mean?''

"You're afraid lightning is going to strike twice and going overboard to stop it. I wish I could say I didn't understand. Or that I could dislike you for it. The truth is I sympathize with what you went through, having no say in what happened to your child. But sooner or later you've got to get over it and move on. Not everyone is out to get you, and you can't control the world. No wonder Dan and Holly ran off. You were holding on so tight you were squeezing the life right out of them."

"Now wait a minute—"

"Let me finish. You're not always right, Jake. And everyone else isn't always wrong. Other people are entitled to an opinion besides yours."

"I never said otherwise."

"You say it by the way you act, as if you're the only one who knows best. It's hard to co-care for a child under those circumstances."

"What are you saying?" He put his hands on his hips and glared at her. "Does this mean our deal is off? That you're taking her? Because the judge said you can't. Even if you could, I'm not going to turn my back on that little girl," he said, pointing to the room where Emma was sleeping.

She shook her head. "I gave my word. To Holly and Dan first, then to you. I can only assure you that my primary concern is now and always has been what's best for that baby. I care about her very much. And I care about—" She met his gaze and her cheeks turned pink.

He remembered what the doctor had said about maintaining emotional distance and figured Rachel was too far gone. He knew that because he loved Emma, too. Studying Rachel's face, he recognized her unease and wondered what she'd been about to say. "What?"

"It doesn't matter." She met his gaze. "You and I have an agreement. Four days at the ranch while you're working. Three days here in the apartment while I am. I have no plans to go back on my word just because you will never trust me."

She looked as if someone—as if *he*—had just pulled the plug and turned off the lights in her world. He wanted to tug her into his arms and tell her she was wrong. But he couldn't.

"So you're saying that until my brother comes back, we'll go on as before?"

"We'll go on, but not as before."

Chapter Ten

The following day Emma's fever was gone. With two more days off, Rachel honored her agreement with Jake and came back to the ranch around noon. Her usual routine was to tidy up the house, do laundry and cook dinner in between tending the baby. While she waited for Jake to come home. Today was no different. Although everything *felt* different.

And she hated the hum of anticipation vibrating through her at the familiar sound of his truck door closing. Then she heard the door from the garage to the service porch open and shut followed by swift, heavy footsteps before Jake walked into the kitchen.

Rachel took one look at his face, the evidence of relief there, and knew what he was thinking. "You wondered whether or not I'd be here, didn't you?"

"I—" He took his hat off and ran his fingers through his hair. "You threw me out of your place last night."

At least he hadn't tried to tell her she was wrong

and she respected him for that. But the fact that he hadn't trusted her, after knowing her, hurt deeply and made her angry.

"I didn't throw you out." She looked up at him, way up. As if she could actually throw him out bodily. But her observation of his tall, lean, powerful build sent shivers skipping over her skin. Unwilling shivers, but that was no consolation. "We agreed that you'd take care of Emma while I'm putting in a shift at the hospital and then go home. I do the same here on the ranch. Since we both have Emma's best interests at heart, no one needs to keep an eye on anyone."

"Yeah."

"But you didn't expect me to keep up my end of the bargain and bring her back to the ranch, did you?"

His eyes narrowed. "Any good lawyer would tell me not to incriminate myself by answering that question. I'll only admit that old habits die hard. But what was your first clue?"

She glanced at the clock on the microwave. "It's only five o'clock. You're wasting a couple hours of perfectly good daylight. That tells me you wanted to see for yourself that I'd brought Emma here as promised."

"Yeah, well—" Looking sheepish, he met her gaze. "Thanks, Rachel."

"There's no reason to thank me." *I only wanted you to trust me.* "It's all part of our deal. Like I said, I'm not a welsher."

She hoped her voice was as carefully casual as she tried to make it. Something had become clear to her since sending him home last night. It had been a month since she'd spent the night without his comforting presence under the same roof. She'd missed him. She missed tripping over his boots in the living room. She missed dishes he left in the sink and crumbs he dropped on the counter. Missing all of that was never part of their deal.

It was proof that she was a spaghetti-spined, weak-willed idiot. She should be relieved to find out there wasn't a snowball's chance in hell he could care, but she wasn't. Every time she looked into his blue eyes, or suppressed the urge to smooth back the lock of black hair slipping over his forehead, or tamped down the temptation to trace the dimple in his chin, she felt the pain slice through her. From the beginning she'd been trying to lead with her head, but Jake Fletcher had launched a sneak attack on her heart.

He let out a long breath. "Where's Emma?"

"On a blanket on the family room floor exploring the infant play gym."

"Doing pull ups?"

She couldn't stop the half smile that sneaked up on her. "Of course. We've already established that she's gifted."

"I know it isn't part of the deal, but would you mind sticking around to keep an eye on her while I take a shower?"

Would she mind? Staying here with the baby she'd come to adore or facing a quiet, empty apartment? That was a no brainer.

"I can stick around."

"Okay. I won't be long."

"Take your time."

He headed through the family room toward the stairs and stopped to see the baby on the floor. From where she stood in the kitchen, Rachel could see his wide shoulders and strong back. Her heart stuttered at the sight. She was so pathetic. If there was a God in heaven, Jake would remain clueless about how she felt. At least she could salvage her pride.

"Hey, little bit," he said, his voice tender as he talked to Emma. "How are you?" The baby responded with a noise that sounded suspiciously like a squeal of pleasure. He laughed and said, "I can't pick you up till I wash off the part of the ranch I brought home with me. Don't you go anywhere till I get back."

Rachel figured that last part was directed at her. Or was she coming down with a strain of Jake Fletcher paranoia? She heaved a big sigh and decided she might as well make herself useful since Emma was content for the moment.

When she'd arrived with the baby that morning, she hadn't found anything out for dinner and had taken a roast from the freezer to defrost. It was one of Jake's favorite meals. After sprinkling the meat with seasonings, she slid it into the preheated oven. Then she peeled potatoes for mashing. She'd learned it was Jake's carbohydrate of choice.

Before she could start on the salad, he came down the stairs. He bent over Emma who was still content on the floor and gave her tummy a tender rub. When he continued to the kitchen, Rachel poured him a glass of iced tea, then handed it to him and he drank gratefully. She watched his Adam's apple bob up and down as the glass's contents disappeared. Why the heck were her insides doing a bump and grind at the masculine sight? And she hated the way her knees went weak at the scent of fresh-scrubbed man that filled the room.

His dark hair was even darker because it was still

wet from his shower. He'd put on clean jeans and a fresh black T-shirt that hugged his chest and upper arms like a second skin. She shivered, remembering how it felt to be held in those strong arms. And before she made a complete fool of herself, it was time for her to hit the road.

"I fixed a roast for you. It should be done in about an hour and a half. The potatoes are peeled and cut up. All you have to do is warm some milk and mash them. Throw in some butter if your cholesterol can handle it. If you want, I'll make a salad before I go."

Go had to be the saddest word in the dictionary. Loneliness settled over her like a shroud.

"Do you really need to rush off?" he asked.

She shrugged. "I've got stuff to do."

"Define 'stuff.'"

"Oh, you know. It's a long drive back to Sweet Spring. And—"

"What?"

"I've got laundry to do. The apartment hasn't had a good cleaning since—" She shook her head. "And I should probably—"

"What? Watch the grass grow? The car rust? Or the ever popular and exciting freezer defrost?"

"I have a frost free freezer." The corners of her mouth curved up, but she refused to give in to the threatening grin.

How did he manage that? She was doing her best to salvage her dignity and pride and he was charming the socks off her. And she was barefoot.

"I have a great idea." He put his hands on his hips. "Why don't you stay for dinner?"

Stay had to be the happiest, most dangerous word in the dictionary. "It's not part of the deal."

"How long are you going to punish me?"

"I'm not doing that," she protested. "Just trying to keep everything on the up and up."

"If you say so. Look at it this way. You'd be doing me a favor. I'm not sure I can handle mashing potatoes and bathing Emma."

"I wouldn't recommend trying to do both at the same time."

His grin nearly dropped her to her knees. "I was hoping to persuade you to help me with the bathing or the mashing—or both."

She blinked. "Who are you and what have you done with Jake Fletcher?"

"What?"

"Jake doesn't use the *H* word."

"A certain blond buttinski showed me the error of my ways."

"What do you know about that?"

"I know I wouldn't mind if you stayed here tonight. I sort of missed the smell of your froufrou soap and stuff."

She narrowed her gaze on him. "If I didn't know better, I'd say you were trying to say you're sorry."

"Nope. Not me."

He was so lying. And so irresistible. And that's why she had to say no. "Thanks, but I really can't."

"Okay, then." His eyes darkened and his mouth compressed into a straight line. Was he actually disappointed?

Just then she heard the front door open. A masculine voice called out, "Jake?"

"Dan?" Jake's eyes widened just before he brushed by her and headed into the other room. Rachel followed. Holly and his brother stood in the entry.

Dan looked uneasy. He was the same height as Jake, a younger, less filled out version of his older brother with the same Fletcher blue eyes and dark hair. "We're back."

Jake stared at him, tension in every angle and line of his face. "Where the hell have you been?"

"Look, bro—"

"Don't you 'bro' me. You took off without a word. I've had the sheriff looking for you. I hired a private investigator. You've got some explaining to do."

The teen glanced from his brother to Rachel, a dark, closed-off expression on his young face. "Why bother? You won't understand."

"Try me."

Rachel stood beside Holly, her arm around the girl's shoulders. She felt the slender brunette's tension and didn't need to see her pale, pretty face to know she was acutely uncomfortable.

"Why don't we all go sit down?" Rachel suggested.

No one moved. You could cut the tension in the air with a cheese slicer. Jake and Dan glared at each other, both of them oozing animosity.

"How's Emma?" Holly asked.

"Better," Rachel answered.

"No thanks to you two," Jake growled. "She's been sick. She saw the doctor yesterday. Do you get how serious it is to have a child depend on you? How irresponsible—" He froze, as if what she'd said had just sunk in. He looked at Rachel, then Holly and finally speared Dan with a glare. "Better? Did you know she was sick?" he asked his brother.

"Yeah." Dan shifted his feet and folded his arms over his chest, tucking his fingertips beneath his arms.

"Rachel told us. She said we better get back if we knew what was good for us."

"You've known where they were all this time?" His glare knifed through her.

Not the whole time, she thought. But Rachel figured this wasn't the time to split hairs. How she'd dreaded this moment. She'd harbored a slim, silly hope that he wouldn't find out. She'd known he would be angry, but the expression of betrayal and contempt on his face nearly dropped her to her knees. The ice in his stare went clear to her soul. With an effort, she looked him straight in the eyes and pulled her shoulders back.

"Yes," she admitted. "But—"

"You knew how concerned I was." His voice vibrated with fury. "Why the hell didn't you tell me?"

"Don't be mad at Rachel," Dan said. "She wanted us to let her tell you."

"We swore her to secrecy." Holly jumped to her defense. "Otherwise you would have come after us and brought us home."

"Damn right," he agreed. "This is where you belong. With your little girl. Don't even get me started on the legal and medical issues." He slammed Dan with a fierce look.

A muscle contracted in Dan's jaw. "Rachel said you guys took Emma to the doctor and she's fine."

"The point is her *father* and *mother* should have been there," Jake ground out. He slid a glare in her direction. "The point is Rachel had no right to keep your whereabouts from me."

"No right?" In a heartbeat, Dan was a hostile and defensive teen. "No right to keep her promise? No right to help me? You can't tell me what to do. Not this time."

"The hell I can't."

Jake and Dan stared at each other like two lions taking each other's measure before pouncing. Rachel could almost feel the testosterone levels in the room getting ready to overflow. She held her breath, wondering if she should step between them.

"This is stupid. I don't have to answer to your brother." Holly stepped forward. "I'm taking Emma, Dan. I need to get out of here. Rachel, can we go back to your apartment? I have to talk to you." She walked past all of them.

"Whatever you have to say, you can say here," Jake said, following.

"All right." Holly's sneaker squealed on the tile as she turned suddenly and met his gaze. "Dan and I have decided to give Emma up for adoption."

Jake poured himself a whiskey—two fingers, neat—while he stood in the kitchen and waited for Dan to clean up. Only a short time had passed since Emma, Holly and Rachel had left. He hadn't been able to think of a way to stop them. He downed the liquor and sucked in a breath as it burned all the way to his gut.

It was happening all over again. History was repeating itself. Only this time it felt even worse. He'd taken care of Emma in a way he'd never been able to care for his own son. Rachel would call it bonding. And it was a bond he didn't plan to break. Not while there was breath in his body.

"Jake?"

He turned at the sound of Dan's voice. He stood in the doorway holding a T-shirt, his jeans slung low on narrow hips. His chest was smooth and not yet filled out. His cheeks and jaw sported whiskers that had been a couple days in the growing. Jake wondered if he'd ever been that young. When he saw the fear in the kid's eyes, he remembered the feeling and knew he had been. Any lingering anger disappeared. He didn't want to fight anymore.

"You hungry?" he asked.

Dan shook his head. "I need to talk to you."

"Before you start, I want you to know I'll support you and Emma and Holly, if she wants."

"You still want us to get married?"

"It would be the best thing for that baby."

"So it doesn't matter what's best for me?"

Jake didn't have an answer.

Dan pulled his shirt on. "I know you'll never forgive me if I don't do what you want. Because you never got a chance to keep your son."

"That's over and done with," Jake said.

"You're wrong. It's not over—not until you forgive Mom for what she did."

Jake's gut knotted with the familiar fury. "She stole my son. How can I forgive that?"

Dan's eyes blazed. "She did what she thought was best. Her heart was in the right place."

"She went behind my back. She lied and cheated to keep him from me."

"She was saving you from yourself."

Jake slammed the empty glass he still held on the kitchen counter. "How can you say that?"

"Because I got a chance to open that window and see how it would be." Dan let out a long breath.

Jake remembered how he'd felt after their mother died when Dan looked to him for everything. "It's called being a grown up, whether you want to or not."

"Think about when you were my age. Think about how it would have felt if you'd married someone you didn't love."

Jake recalled seeing the woman who'd borne his son, comparing notes, figuring out what had happened. He'd been furious about the deception, but that was the strongest emotion he'd felt. He hadn't missed his son's mother. Not the way he missed Rachel when she was gone for twelve hours. Or when he was away from her while working on the ranch.

But how could he feel that way about a woman who would keep something so important from him? Especially when she knew this was a hot button for him?

"Marrying someone you don't love would be hard," he admitted.

"It would be wrong." Dan folded his arms over his chest and leaned against the refrigerator. "Holly and I found out a lot while we were on our own. We couldn't get jobs that pay well—"

"I can afford to support you, Dan. This ranch is as much yours as mine."

"But it's not what I want." He shook his head. "And it's not just that. I want—*we* want—to go to college. Holly's going to apply for student loans and figure out how to make it work financially." Dan rubbed the back of his neck. "I want the experience of going away to school. I want that athletic scholarship. I earned it. That felt pretty damn good. I don't want to take classes at night and get my degree at the local college like you did. Holly and I found out we can't do the things we want with a baby."

"You should have thought of that before having sex." Jake knew he was being harsh and didn't much care.

Dan nodded. "You're right. But I didn't. That's why it's so important to think it through now. Holly and I need to deal with the fact that eventually we would resent Emma. That's not fair to her."

"A man faces up to his responsibilities."

"I guess I'm not as good a man as you are."

In spite of playing devil's advocate, everything Dan said struck a chord deep inside Jake. He'd been the same age when his son was born. Would the boy be doing as well as he was now if he hadn't had the stability of a family right from the beginning? Suddenly Jake was tired clear to the bone, as if he'd been swimming upstream for years.

But he had to take one last shot. "You're young, Danny. You don't know what kind of man you'll be until you're tested. How do you know marriage won't work? A family would be best for Emma—"

"I agree. But Holly and I decided *we* would be a mistake. How can a divorce be good for Emma?"

"You can't love Holly?"

"I care about her, but I don't think I know what love is."

At Dan's age, Jake hadn't, either. And his rage at his mother's betrayal in the name of love had kept him from wanting further experience with the emotion. But Rachel and Emma had sneaked in under his defenses.

"What about Emma?" Jake asked. "How can you not love your daughter?"

"I love Emma enough to let her go. I love her enough to give her a chance at a stable family—the kind of life I can't give her right now." Dan stared at him, his eyes bleak and begging for understanding. "I know in my gut this is right, Jake. Holly and I tried.

Sometimes knowing what doesn't work is more important than knowing what does. We found out we don't belong together for the long haul. Thanks to Rachel. We owe her a lot.''

"Do we?'' Jake's gut twisted painfully. Rachel had flinched as if struck when he'd said she had no right to keep Dan's secret.

"I do,'' Dan said. "She's a pretty special lady. Helping Holly the way she did. Over and over she asked us to let her tell you where we were but we wouldn't. I'm sorry, Jake. But think about it. She kept her promise to us. That can't have been easy. You can be kind of intimidating.''

"You think?''

"Yeah. And I don't think you get her at all. If she can keep her word to Holly and me, she'd do it for anyone.''

Jake looked at his brother and blew out a long breath. Whether he agreed or not, the kid had obviously given a lot of thought to this.

"How did you get so smart?'' Jake asked.

One corner of Dan's mouth tilted up in a crooked grin. "You can thank Rachel.''

"There's something you need to know, Dan.'' Jake met his brother's gaze. "I won't try and change your mind about giving up your rights to Emma.''

"I appreciate that.''

"Did you know the court ordered Rachel and me to share custody?''

Dan nodded. "We talked to her a few times and she told us everything that was going on.''

"What you don't know is that I've gotten pretty attached to that little girl.'' No one had to tell him Rachel was, too. "She's my niece, but I feel as if she's my little girl. I won't let her go—not to strangers. And before you say anything, this has nothing to do with my son or the past. I love her," he said simply.

Dan blinked. "Are you saying you want to adopt her?"

"Yeah. Do you have a problem with that?"

"I would never ask—"

"I'm telling you how it's going to be." When he heard the words, he smiled. "It's what I want, if it's all right with you."

"More than all right. I have to admit it would be a relief to know she's with you."

"Why's that?"

"You're family," he said with a shrug. "And I know you did all right by me. She'll be in good hands."

"Thanks," Jake said, his voice thick with emotion. He held out his hand. When Dan took it, he pulled his brother into a bear hug. "That means a lot to me."

Jake knew what he was doing was right. As Dan had said, it felt right. "Do you think Holly will be okay with me adopting Emma?"

Dan stepped away. "My guess would be no. She talked about wanting to give the baby to Rachel. It's one of the things Holly and I argued about." Dan looked serious. "I want Emma to be with you."

Jake wanted that, too. But he had a feeling right about now Holly was asking Rachel to raise her daughter. And Rachel would agree.

They were headed for a showdown. Which one of them would be left standing?

Chapter Eleven

Rachel sat on the couch feeding the baby after her bath. Holly was in a wing chair across from her, keeping her distance. What was going through her mind? Rachel was strung so tight she felt as if she might snap, and she tried to relax. She didn't want Emma to feel the tension. She loved this child so much. Between that and thoughts of Jake, her heart felt like it had been drop-kicked down desperation lane.

Rachel forced a cheerfulness into her voice that she wasn't even close to feeling. "So how did it go? Did you like being on your own? I should say, you and Dan being on your own."

"It's not what I thought it would be at all." Holly finally met her gaze. "The best jobs we could get were working nights at Wal-Mart. Do you know how much food costs? And rent? And utilities?"

"It's expensive to live," Rachel agreed, glancing down at the infant in her arms.

"I priced disposable diapers for Emma. They cost

a lot. So does baby food. Then I thought about who would take care of her while we worked. There was no way we could afford that and everything else, too.''

''I understand,'' Rachel said. Somehow she knew Holly needed to get all this off her chest before they got to the real issue.

''I thought Dan loved me and everything would be perfect.'' Her gaze was bleak. ''But that's not the way it was. We were tired and snapping at each other all the time. He was on my case about every cent I spent.'' Her blue eyes flashed. ''He's just like his brother.''

Rachel didn't think that was such a bad thing, but figured this wasn't the best time to say so. ''I see.''

Holly squirmed in the chair. ''Some day Emma will have to go to school. She'll need clothes. Kids make fun of you if your clothes and shoes come from thrift stores. And heaven forbid they don't match.''

Rachel just nodded her understanding. ''Jake wants to support the three of you so you can be a family. Did you know that?''

Holly's gaze locked with hers and the hostility was unmistakable. ''And have him tell us what to do all the time? No way.''

''He wouldn't do that.''

''No? You saw how he was earlier, telling us where we belonged. That we ran away from our responsibilities. We took off for a while and had more responsibilities than ever.''

''He's a good man and he cares about all of you.'' Rachel looked down when the baby squirmed. She removed the bottle from the baby's mouth and lifted Emma to her shoulder for a burp. ''You should have seen Jake with the baby. He was a hoot changing diapers at first—''

''Jake changed her?''

Rachel nodded. ''He had to. Remember the court gave us both temporary custody, and he took care of her while I was at work. He bathed her, too. Although the first time I thought he was going to have a stroke or heart failure. But he got pretty good at it. He walked the floor with her. And he got excellent at dialing the phone and ordering take out.''

Holly didn't crack a smile. ''How can you defend him? He was practically yelling at you for keeping your promise not to tell where we were.''

''He was just surprised.'' In a pig's eye. What Rachel had done was nothing less than what he'd expected. But the way he'd looked at her— She shivered. Would she ever feel warm again?

''There you go,'' Holly said, her eyes narrowing as she stared.

''What?''

''Every time you talk about him, you get a weird, sort of soft expression on your face. You didn't fall for him, did you, Rachel?''

''I'm just trying to be fair,'' she lied. ''He's not as bad as you think.''

''Yes, he is. And I don't want anything from him.''

The baby squirmed and squeaked, taking her attention from the teen. Rachel looked from Emma to Holly. ''Do you want to hold her?''

The young girl shifted away as she shook her head. ''I have to tell you something. Promise you won't hate me.''

Making promises had backfired on her, Rachel

thought. But she figured she didn't have much more to lose. "What is it?"

"As bad as it was with the fighting and no money, I was glad Emma wasn't with us."

"That's understandable. You wanted her safe—"

Holly shook her head. "No. When I first found out I was pregnant, I was scared—but glad. I thought someone would finally love me. But that's not how it was. It was nothing but work. All she does is eat and cry. I changed diapers and was tired all the time. I liked working, talking to people. I liked not having to take a diaper bag with me everywhere I went. It felt like I was free." Her gaze was pleading. "Do you hate me?"

Rachel sighed. Holly was a child herself. She wasn't ready to be a mother. "Of course not."

"Dan wants his brother to raise Emma."

Rachel's heart seemed to stop for a second and when it started again it slammed against her ribs. "I see. So you both agree about giving her up?"

"Yes." Holly's lips quivered. "I can understand now what my mother went through. She left me at the bus station. She said after the bus was gone, a policeman would take care of me. I remember how scared I was. But that was nothing compared to how scary it is when you have a baby depending on you. And I see now what she was going through and how hard it must have been to make it with me. And she tried. I know she did."

"I'm sure she loves you very much," Rachel said.

The girl met her gaze. "I don't want Emma to see me walk away because I can't take care of her. Adoption is the best solution. While she's too young to remember. While she's a baby and someone will want her. Anyone except Jake.''

"He's her uncle. He would be the logical choice. And I know he wants her.''

"What about you? Don't you want her?''

"Of course I do. I love her,'' she said simply, as she snuggled the infant in her arms. She could no more resist falling in love with this child than she could flap her arms and fly to the moon. "But, think about—''

"I want you to have her.''

Rachel met her gaze as emotions crashed through her. Happiness and heartbreak. She wanted this baby more than anything. But she knew Jake would never back off.

"I don't think Jake would go along with that.''

"He doesn't get a say.''

"Somehow I don't think that will stop him.''

"You mean he'll throw his weight around.'' Holly met her gaze. "That's exactly why I don't think he should raise her.''

"You and Dan are going to have to sign away your rights to Emma. And before you do that, I want you to have some counseling.''

"Okay, but we won't change our minds. This feels right. In fact, I thought about giving Emma to you before she was born.''

"You did?''

"Yeah. When you were away in New Orleans with your friends for your birthday. The idea popped into my head that you'd be a good mother to my baby.''

Rachel shook her head. It was too weird. "Holly, think about this carefully. Jake is a blood relative. He's a good man. The ranch is a wonderful place to bring up a child. He's really not as bad as you think.''

"But he's not a woman."

"No, he's not." That was an understatement. Rachel remembered the feel of being pressed to his wide chest and muscular thighs. His big hands running up and down her back. The scrape of his five-o'clock shadow across her cheek. He was definitely all man.

"Emma is a girl. She needs a woman to raise her." Holly leaned forward, her gaze intense. "She needs a mom."

The bleak look in Holly's eyes connected with the yearning inside Rachel. She'd always wanted a mother. The statement took all the starch out of any further protest she'd planned to make. No way on God's green earth could she turn down this request. Especially when she loved the baby so much.

"Raising this little girl would be a privilege and a joy."

"Then it's settled."

Rachel shook her head. "Not by a long shot. We'll get some legal advice. And I'll do my best to get custody. But Jake will fight me."

"Then you'll just have to beat him," Holly said.

And what about beating her feelings for him? Rachel thought. Emma had been the glue holding them together. Fighting him for custody would cost her any slim chance she'd had with him.

Rachel had always felt her mother had chosen her father over her child. Now she realized she'd been wrong, carrying around the impressions of a child. A child who'd become a woman with grown-up choices to make. She wished it wasn't so.

And this choice had never been part of her wish.

Jake heard the doorbell ring. He'd been waiting for her. It seemed like years since he'd seen her instead of a couple days. He opened the door. Rachel stood there holding the baby carrier.

"Rachel."

"I wasn't sure you'd be here. I guess you got the message I left on your cell phone."

He nodded and stepped aside, allowing her to pass in front of him. "I was surprised when you said you were coming over." He looked at the baby, surprised again that she'd brought Emma with her.

"I have to talk to you," she said.

He nodded. "Let me take her for you."

When he put his hand on the carrier handle, their fingers brushed. Rachel pulled away as if she'd touched a hot oven rack. That didn't stop him from feeling a sizzle of awareness. She felt it, too. He saw it in the way her cheeks flushed, followed by a deliberate shifting of the diaper bag on her shoulder, a move meant to cover her reaction to him. He was glad she was affected. Glad to know he wasn't the only one. Because he'd tried and failed to ignore the way he felt about her.

"Let's go in the family room," he said, staring at Emma. He'd missed her. Since they'd negotiated their arrangement, he hadn't gone a day without seeing her. It felt like months instead of just a few days ago. "She looks good."

"She's great."

Her sandals clicked on the tile entry as she followed him. In the other room, she sat on the sofa and he took a chair at a right angle to her, settling the baby carrier on the rug between them.

"Where's Dan?" she asked.

"He's doing errands in town. Getting ready to go

away to school." He met her gaze. "Holly got a job. I've seen her in The Fast Lane."

They'd had a chance to talk. He'd felt some barriers go down on both sides.

"Tip her big. She's saving every penny she can. She's been accepted to a college in North Texas, but her student loan hasn't been approved yet. I co-signed for her."

His mouth curved up. "There's a surprise."

He wanted to tell her about his plans to help Holly, but knew she would think he had ulterior motives. He needed to play his hand carefully.

She shrugged. "We're keeping our fingers crossed that it comes through soon. Otherwise she's going to take classes locally and try again next semester."

"And stay with you?"

She nodded. "Too many kids who age out of foster care wind up on the streets, completely unprepared for the real world. A high percentage don't even graduate from high school. She beat those odds. And I'll help her beat the rest as long as she needs me to."

"You didn't come here to tell me that," he said, resting his forearms on his knees as he leaned forward.

"No. I thought you'd want to see Emma." Her gaze lifted to his. "And I wanted to tell you that Holly asked me to take her. I'm going to try to get permanent custody."

Holly had told him. "I see."

"Jake, I didn't take Holly under my wing to bug you. No one understands why I'd turn my life upside down to take care of a baby. But it didn't feel like upside down to me because it was only going to be temporary." She blinked moisture from her lashes.

"Now it doesn't feel upside down because I fell in love with her."

Something twisted in his chest. God, he didn't want to hurt her. "You know I have the stronger claim."

She nodded. "But I have to try. And it's not just for Holly."

"Then what?"

"I know you'll never understand why I couldn't tell you where Holly and Dan were." She met his gaze, her own naked with the truth. "I didn't do it to hurt you. Unless there was a crisis or some reason you needed to know their location, I agreed not to say anything to you. Look, Jake, they were on the edge. I was concerned that they might do something irresponsible."

"You think taking off like they did was responsible?"

"Of course not. But it could have been worse."

He ran his fingers through his hair. "Yeah. I know all about worse. But, Dan is my brother. That makes Emma my family," he said.

"Compatible DNA doesn't qualify you as the better caregiver."

"It's all I've got. How about you?"

"I made a promise when Holly begged me to try to get custody."

"She's just a kid."

"A kid who's mature enough to know she's not ready to be a mother." Rachel let out a long breath. "And she doesn't want to make the same mistakes her mother did."

He nodded. "Dan and I had a long talk. He told me about Holly's background."

"Then you can appreciate what a courageous choice

she's making so that her child won't experience the same pain and rejection.''

He nodded. "I can give Emma everything.''

"Everything but your complete trust. Is that the best environment for a child?''

"Nothing is perfect,'' he countered.

"Love is. In it's purest form. Holly and Dan love their child enough to let her go. To give her the opportunity for a better life.''

"And you think you can give her that?''

She shrugged. "I only know one thing for sure. At first, I was protecting Holly's place in this child's life. But somewhere along the way, I fell in love with Emma. If I'm fortunate enough to win custody of her, all I can give her is my love and the best life I can provide.''

"Me, too.'' He stood. "Plus, I can give her a sense of where she came from. Her family.''

Rachel stood, too. "Okay. I just wanted you to hear it from me. Because Holly asked me. And because I can't stand the thought of losing someone else I love.''

He looked startled. "Rachel, I—''

"It's just the truth. And so is this. I care about you, Jake. A lot. You're a man with the courage of his convictions. A man who will go to the mat for the people he loves. I know you'll never forgive me for lying to you. But I'll never forgive myself if I don't try to get custody of Emma. Whether you believe me or not, I had to say all of this to your face.''

She drew in a shuddering breath, then quickly picked up the baby carrier and walked to the door.

Jake was blown away. By what she'd said and the fact that she'd let him know face to face about her custody challenge. Everything up-front. No going behind his back. She was a hell of a woman. Dan was right. He hadn't understood that Rachel was a by-the-book sort of woman. But he knew it now. Because he was in love with her.

He hurried after her. He needed to tell her. But when he got to the door and opened it, he heard her car start and he saw taillights as she drove away.

"Rachel—"

But she couldn't hear him. Even if she could, would she listen? He doubted it. And it was his own damn fault. He'd driven her away.

Chapter Twelve

Rachel answered the knock on her door and saw Jordan and Ashley standing there. "What are you guys doing here?"

"When I called earlier, you sounded like you could use some cheering up." Jordan tossed a strand of dark hair over her shoulder as she walked into the apartment.

Ashley held out a bottle of wine. "We brought spirits."

"Very funny." Rachel closed the door. Normally the sight of Ash's curly red hair and the twinkle in Jordan's warm brown eyes were enough to cheer her. Not tonight.

"There's nothing funny about chocolate." Jordan flaunted a plastic grocery bag bulging at the sides. "Among other carbohydrates guaranteed to make you do the happy dance—at least temporarily."

Ashley looked at the baby paraphernalia scattered

around the apartment living room. "I don't hear Emma. Is she here?"

Rachel shook her head. "She's with Jake. According to the arrangement we worked out."

Her two friends went into the kitchen and helped themselves to long-stemmed glasses and a corkscrew. Rachel was glad they helped themselves because she was in no mood to play hostess. They rooted in the cupboards for serving bowls and the rustling of plastic bags drowned out a depressing country western song about a man who hit his stride when he hit the road.

When Jordan had called her a little while ago, Rachel had tried to disguise her mood. But her friend knew her too well and guessed that she was down in the dumps. Her throat closed with emotion. She had no right to be dispirited when she was lucky enough to call these two bright, beautiful, warm and caring women her best friends. If she lost Emma, she knew Jordan and Ashley wouldn't let her become an eccentric old recluse who adopted stray cats and collected newspapers.

Jordan handed her a glass of red wine. "Okay, I want the truth, the whole truth and nothing but the truth. Why are you so unperky?"

Rachel narrowed her eyes. "Is that even a word?"

"Don't ask me." Jordan shrugged. "I changed my major in college three times but not once was it English."

"'Un' is a definite negative. I think you can put it in front of anything and it works. In a bad way." Ashley set a bowl of potato chips on the coffee table. "My guess is that Jake Fletcher is doing something *un*imaginably *un*gentlemanly."

"For once let us mother you." Jordan put her arm around Rachel's shoulders.

"Speaking of mothers," Ashley said frowning. "I thought Holly and Dan were back. Why is Emma with Jake instead of here with her mother?"

"Holly's working at The Fast Lane. And my temporary custody arrangement with Jake stands until we go back to court." Her friends knew the whole story except the most recent highlights. "But Holly and Dan decided to give the baby up." When they opened their mouths to bombard her with questions, she held up her hand for silence. "Jake filed a petition for adoption. I counterfiled."

"You fell in love with Emma after I told you not to," Ashley guessed.

"As you pointed out so eloquently—this is me. Besides, I think it was too late the moment I laid eyes on her," Rachel said. "Holly asked because she doesn't want Jake to have her. But the truth is it's something I really and truly want to do."

Rachel knew if a miracle happened and she was granted custody, she'd have to work hard not to let Emma feel a sense of abandonment like she'd felt. But she'd finally learned to let go of the past. The most important thing was to move forward and play the hand life dealt. She would do her best to convey that lesson to Emma.

"So Holly still doesn't like Jake," Jordan commented, thoughtfully tapping her lips. "Come to think of it, you weren't too crazy about him, either. The adjectives *stubborn, opinionated* and *controlling* come to mind."

Ashley sat on the couch. "For an un-English major it's impressive that Jordan knows the word adjective.

But she's right. I was also under the impression that you had some reservations about Jake.''

"Why would you think that?''

Jordan huffed out a breath. "Because you said, and I quote, 'I don't like Jake Fletcher.' Unquote. So what gives?''

"He's not as controlling, stubborn and opinionated as I first thought.'' She mulled over that statement. "And he has very good reasons for his behavior.''

"That sounds like you're defending him.'' Jordan raised one delicate, dark eyebrow. "Would you care to explain this complete about-face?''

"I've gotten to know him.'' And then some, she thought. A couple of toe-curling kisses came to mind and she hoped her friends would think the heat in her cheeks was a side effect of her wine. "I sort of had to because of the temporary custody agreement.''

"Define 'know,''' Jordan said. "Is it 'know' in the biblical sense?''

"If you're asking if I've slept with him, that's a definite negative.''

"Because you didn't want to?'' Ashley sat forward, eagerly waiting for an answer.

"No. I mean yes.'' She sighed, then drained the remainder of the wine in her glass. "I'm not sure what I'm saying.''

"And you're a bad liar,'' Jordan said. "Your bluffing isn't too good, either. He kissed you, didn't he?''

"Yeah.''

"And you liked it, didn't you?'' Ashley asked.

"Yeah.''

"You're in love with him,'' her two friends said together.

"Not true." Rachel shook her head. "You guys know I don't fall in love."

"From what you've told us, Jake Fletcher is a good man. At least this time you picked a guy who's worthy of you," Jordan observed, ignoring the protest.

"I didn't pick him. He sort of appeared. And I'm not in love with him." Rachel hoped if she said it enough, it would be true.

"And he's different from the strays you normally bring home. He's not trying to con you out of something," Ashley pointed out.

"If you're talking money, that's true. But he wants the baby as much as I do."

Jordan and Ashley looked at each other, then met her gaze. "Have you thought about that night in New Orleans?" Jordan asked. "You wished for a baby and along came Emma. How weird is that?"

"When I made that wish, subconsciously I was thinking fall in love, marry, do the wild thing and get pregnant."

"One out of four isn't bad," Jordan said.

"I'm not in love," she protested. It was lip service because she knew they were right.

Ashley smiled. "Who said anything about love?"

"Has to be because the other three don't apply. I will only admit to falling head over heels for Emma. But she's his niece which makes my chances of adopting her slim to none."

"Maybe not." Ashley tucked a strand of curly hair behind her ear. "Your wish could come true."

"I'll find out in court tomorrow. The judge is handing down her ruling."

If by some miracle it went in her favor, she would lose Jake. The thought produced a pain so deep and

sharp it nearly drove her to her knees. If she got
Emma, Jake would never forgive her and she'd never
be whole. If he got Em, he'd turn away from her because she was nothing more than an interfering buttinski. Losing them both would break her heart.

She was in love with Jake.

It was suddenly clear to her that she'd always
picked men she couldn't trust and respect. In essence,
she'd taken care not to choose love not realizing it
chooses you. From out of nowhere, Jake had sashayed
into her life. And suddenly someone else's happiness
was more important than her own.

Is this the way her mother had felt about her father?
For the first time Rachel could understand why it was
so important for her to be with him. And how torn she
must have been about leaving her daughter behind.
She'd only done it because she'd thought she was
coming back.

Rachel didn't see that there was a solution in this
case. The judge's ruling had forced she and Jake to
work together for the sake of the baby. And because
of his past, losing Emma might destroy him. How
could she do that to the man she loved?

With Emma asleep in the carrier between Rachel
and her attorney, the three of them sat at the table
facing the judge's bench. Across the aisle Jake sat beside his lawyer. Holly had told her Dan had left for
school the day before, right after the two of them had
signed the papers severing their parental rights.

The moment of truth was near and Rachel rubbed
her sweaty palms together. She felt like she was going
to throw up.

The door behind them opened and closed and footsteps sounded. Then Holly sat beside her. "Rachel, I have to talk to you."

"I thought you decided it would be easier if you weren't here. Are you all right?" Rachel met her gaze.

"I'm fine. Better than fine." Holly glanced to the table where Jake sat. "I just found out I have the money I'll need for college."

"You mean the loan was approved? That's fantastic."

Holly shook her head. "It's not the loan. Jake's giving me the money. He set up a fund at the bank."

Rachel was stunned. She turned and looked at Jake, dressed in his suit and tie. His gaze, swirling with intensity, locked with hers. Her heart did a triple back flip in her chest. If only…

No, she wasn't going there. Hope was not her friend; it let you down then kicked you to the curb. "I don't understand. Do you think he's trying to buy your approval for the adoption?"

"I might have thought that once. But not anymore. He comes into The Fast Lane for dinner a lot. He's a good tipper, by the way. But we've talked and he seemed interested in my plans. He asked what I wanted to do with my life. I told him I plan to get my degree, then study law."

"I didn't know that."

She shrugged. "I've taken an interest in family law."

Rachel squeezed her hand. "You can do anything you set your mind to."

"That's what Jake said. Thanks to him, now I can set my mind to something that will make a difference."

"And you're sure his timing doesn't make this suspicious?" she asked, glancing over her shoulder.

"I wasn't supposed to find out until later today. The bank manager came into The Fast Lane for an early lunch and started talking about how lucky I was. He thought Jake had already told me." Holly looked down at the fingers twisting together in Rachel's lap. "I don't think Jake wanted us to find out until after the hearing."

"Have you changed your mind about him having the baby?"

"He's not what I thought at all. He's a really good guy." Holly glanced up, conflict swirling in her eyes. "I think Emma would be lucky to have either of you. I just thought you should know." She stood up. "I have to get back to work now."

Rachel was too stunned to say anything as she watched the teen walk out of the courtroom. Before she could discuss this with Kara, a shuffling sound drew her attention to the front of the room.

"All rise for Judge Olivia Edwards."

Dressed in her black robe, the judge swept in and took her seat behind the bench. "Everyone be seated." She looked at them over the granny glasses perched on the end of her nose. "I've looked over the paperwork for Manning versus Fletcher in the matter of the minor Emma Fletcher. The teenage parents have been counseled and have subsequently signed away their rights to the infant." She folded her hands and settled them on her desk as she stared down from the bench. "Often in the adoption process prospective parents obtain letters of reference from friends attesting to their character and fitness. But a friend is unlikely to tell the unvarnished truth. I've always thought the tradi-

tional wedding question was more fair—is there anyone present who knows why this adoption shouldn't
take place? Miss Manning, can you think of any reason why Jake Fletcher shouldn't be allowed to adopt
his niece?''

Rachel's stomach clenched with disappointment.
She figured the judge had already made up her mind
and she'd lost Emma. But she couldn't say anything
less than the truth.

She glanced across the aisle, then stood. Taking a
deep breath, she met the judge's gaze. "Before I got
to really know Jake, I didn't like him very much, even
though I knew he'd raised his younger brother after
both of their parents died. I thought he was stubborn,
opinionated and controlling. But I'm also aware that
children are a product of their environment. They learn
what they live. Dan Fletcher is a fine young man. He's
shown remarkable courage in a difficult situation and
the strength to make a painful choice. He learned to
be the man he is from Jake.'' She took a shuddering
breath. "Thanks to Your Honor's last ruling, I was
forced to become acquainted with Jake on a more personal level. I've found him to be patient and loving
with the baby. Without a single qualm, I can say that
Jake Fletcher will make a fine father.''

"I see.'' The judge looked at Jake. "Your turn. Can
you think of any reason Miss Manning shouldn't have
custody of the minor infant?''

Jake stared at Rachel with a look in his eyes that
she couldn't read. Then he stood and buttoned his suit
coat. "My brother reminded me that neither he nor
Holly were raised by their mother and missed the maternal influence. From day one, Rachel has been telling
me that children need a mother. She's been wonderful

with Emma.'' He let out a long breath. ''She's honest, loyal and the finest woman it's ever been my honor to know.''

Rachel's jaw nearly dropped. Did he mean it? This was a court of law. They hadn't sworn on the Bible. But wouldn't lightning strike if he wasn't telling the truth?

''Hold it right there, Jake,'' the judge said. ''You've got nothing bad to say about the woman opposing you for custody of your niece?''

''Livvie, you asked me if there's any reason Rachel shouldn't have custody. The answer is no. She's perfect.''

''It's 'Your Honor' to you while you're in this court.'' The judge's glance slid from Jake to Rachel and she shook her head. ''I wish there was a statute of limitation on stupidity. It would make my job so much easier, not to mention my docket less crowded. A blind person could tell you two are crazy about each other.''

She clasped her hands together and leaned forward. ''Okay, here's the deal. Jake, I'm granting your petition for adoption. Now I'm going to clear the courtroom, and I want you and Miss Manning to stay here and talk. If it was in my power I would sentence you to life with each other because it's clear to everyone but the two of you that it would be poetic justice.''

Rachel's head was pounding even before the judge banged her gavel signaling court adjourned. The room echoed with the sound of papers being gathered, briefcases snapping shut, shuffling feet, the door swinging closed. Then she was alone with Jake.

Warily, she looked over at him. ''Did you mean what you said about me?''

"Yes." He crossed the aisle and stopped a whisper away. "Did you mean what you said about me?"

She blinked away the tears in her eyes and looked up at him. "Yes."

He frowned. "I need to know something. Holly told you about the college money, didn't she?"

"Yes."

"Damn it."

"What's wrong?" she asked.

"Is that why you said what you said?"

"No. I said it because it's the truth."

"How could I have ever doubted you?" He shook his head. "You made me sound like I have wings and a halo even though you want Emma as much as I do."

"It was always the right thing for Emma to be with you." She drew in a shuddering breath. "Once I knew Holly approved of you adopting Emma, my promise to her was fulfilled. It's as simple as that."

"But you love her, too—"

"With all my heart—" The tears she'd been holding back spilled over. Rachel covered her face with her hands and spun away. Sobs shook her as big hands curved around her upper arms and turned her. The next thing she knew, she was folded against a wide chest and wrapped in Jake's strong arms. It was a place she never wanted to leave, but she knew she had to.

She lifted her cheek from his chest. "Jake, let me go."

"Nope. Not this time."

"What do you mean?" she asked, looking up at him.

"And be in contempt of court? We've been ordered to talk about us and that's what I intend to do." His gaze slid over her. "The day you came out to the ranch to tell me you were challenging my adoption petition, I realized something.''

''What did you realize?'' she asked, hope expanding inside her.

''After you left in such a hurry,'' he said, ''I decided to wait until after the custody hearing was over. I was going to break the news about Holly's college money, too. I didn't want there to be any doubt.''

''About what?'' she asked with growing impatience.

''That I'm in love with you.''

He was in love with her? And he'd known for a while? And let her suffer? She thought about all the sleepless nights since she'd seen him. All the doubt and uncertainty. All the unhappiness thinking she would never be with the man she loved.

''I love you, too. Which proves the judge was right about that whole statute on stupidity,'' she snapped. ''I've been completely miserable. Why the heck didn't you say something sooner?''

He grinned, not at all put out by her show of temper. The gentle, seductive way he was moving his hands up and down her arms was turning her pique into something more like passion. ''I wanted to court you.''

''Is that a pun?'' she asked.

He shrugged. ''I mean good, old-fashioned spooning. I planned to wait an appropriate amount of time, so you didn't think it was about Emma.'' He glanced at the baby in the infant seat beside her, looking up at them with her wide blue eyes. ''Then I figured to pursue you until you realized you love me as much as I love you.''

''How can you love me when you don't trust me?'' she said, needing to be sure. Needing him to be sure.

"I trust you implicitly. I disagreed with you, but how can I not love you for keeping your promise to Holly and Dan?"

"But you've been through so much. How can you—"

He cupped her face in his palms and brushed the tears from her cheeks with his thumbs. "I know what you're thinking. And I'll always have regrets about my son. But we don't get through life without regrets. He's doing well and that's the most important thing. My mother knew I didn't have the maturity to raise a child. She did what she thought was right for both of us. Wrong thing, right reason. I understand it now and I can finally let it go. Thanks to you and Dan. I'm proud of him."

"You should be. You'll do a wonderful job with Emma."

"I can't do it by myself. Emma needs a mother," he said.

His blue eyes darkened and he brushed his thumb across her lips. Lowering his head, he touched his mouth to hers. In the joining, she felt his trust and love. She knew everything he'd said had come straight from his heart.

When he pulled back, he met her gaze. "I choose you, Rachel. I need you to help me. I love you. I want you to marry me and be the mother of our child."

"I love you." The words echoed through the courtroom, a place where the truth was sacred. Happiness bubbled up inside her, pushing out sadness and uncertainty. "Nothing would make me happier than to be your wife and the mother of our child."

He smiled, a tender expression softening his features. "I think I've loved you from the moment I dropped by your apartment and saw you in your pajamas. Emma couldn't have a more wonderful mother.''

"Or father."

Looking at Emma, smiling her toothless smile as if she approved of her new parents, Rachel knew her wish for a baby had come true. She remembered the Gypsy's words—one wish is enough if it's the right one. Even though she'd been forbidden to ask for a man, Jake had shown up on her doorstep because of the baby.

And he was definitely the right one.

*   *   *   *   *

Don't miss Ashley's story,
FLIRTING WITH THE BOSS (RS #1708),
the next book in Teresa Southwick's
enchanting miniseries,
IF WISHES WERE…

Available February 2004!

SILHOUETTE *Romance*®

Discover what happens
when wishes come true
in

if Wishes Were...

A brand-new miniseries
from reader favorite

Teresa Southwick

Three friends, three birthdays,
three loves of a lifetime!

BABY, OH BABY!
(Silhouette Romance #1704, Available January 2004)

FLIRTING WITH THE BOSS
(Silhouette Romance #1708, Available February 2004)

AN HEIRESS ON HIS DOORSTEP
(Silhouette Romance #1712, Available March 2004)

Available at your favorite retail outlet.

Visit Silhouette at www.eHarlequin.com   SRIWW

If you enjoyed what you just read,
then we've got an offer you can't resist!

Take 2 bestselling love stories FREE!

Plus get a FREE surprise gift!

Clip this page and mail it to Silhouette Reader Service

IN U.S.A.	IN CANADA
3010 Walden Ave.	P.O. Box 609
P.O. Box 1867	Fort Erie, Ontario
Buffalo, N.Y. 14240-1867	L2A 5X3

YES! Please send me 2 free Silhouette Romance® novels and my free surprise gift. After receiving them, if I don't wish to receive anymore, I can return the shipping statement marked cancel. If I don't cancel, I will receive 6 brand-new novels every month, before they're available in stores! In the U.S.A., bill me at the bargain price of $21.34 per shipment plus 25¢ shipping and handling per book and applicable sales tax, if any*. In Canada, bill me at the bargain price of $24.68 plus 25¢ shipping and handling per book and applicable taxes**. That's the complete price and a savings of at least 10% off the cover prices—what a great deal! I understand that accepting the 2 free books and gift places me under no obligation ever to buy any books. I can always return a shipment and cancel at any time. Even if I never buy another book from Silhouette, the 2 free books and gift are mine to keep forever.

209 SDN DU9H
309 SDN DU9J

Name	(PLEASE PRINT)	
Address	Apt.#	
City	State/Prov.	Zip/Postal Code

* Terms and prices subject to change without notice. Sales tax applicable in N.Y.
** Canadian residents will be charged applicable provincial taxes and GST.
  All orders subject to approval. Offer limited to one per household and not valid to
  current Silhouette Romance® subscribers.
  ® are registered trademarks of Harlequin Books S.A., used under license.

SROM03   ©1998 Harlequin Enterprises Limited

COMING NEXT MONTH

#1706 ONE BACHELOR TO GO—Nicole Burnham
Marrying the Boss's Daughter

Emily Winters had successfully married off all of her dad's eligible executives except one: Jack Devon, the devilishly handsome VP of Global Strategy. A business trip was her chance to learn more about the man behind the mysterious demeanor. But after sharing close quarters—and a few passionate kisses—Emily was ready to marry Jack off...
to herself!

#1707 WYATT'S READY-MADE FAMILY—
Patricia Thayer
The Texas Brotherhood

When rodeo rider Wyatt Gentry came face-to-face with sassy single mom Maura Wells, she was holding a rifle on him! The startled, sexy cowboy soon convinced her to put down the gun and give him a job on her ranch. Now if he could only convince the love-wary beauty that he was the man who could teach her and her two kids how to trust again....

#1708 FLIRTING WITH THE BOSS—Teresa Southwick
If Wishes Were...

Everybody should have money and power, right? But despite her birthday wish, all that Ashley Gallagher got was Max Bentley, her boss's heartbreaker of a grandson. She had to convince him to stay in town long enough to save the company. And love-smitten Ashley was more than ready to use any means necessary to see that Max stayed put!

#1709 SAVED BY THE BABY—Linda Goodnight

Julianna Reynolds would do anything to save her dying daughter—even ask Sheriff Tate McIntyre to father another child. Trouble was, she'd never told him about their *first* child! Shocked, Tate would only agree to her plan if Julianna became his wife. But could their new baby be the miracle they needed to save their daughter *and* their marriage of convenience?

SRCNM0104